I0638680

The Miracle of the Bread
and Other Stories

Other book collections by Arthur Porges:

Three Porges Parodies and a Pastiche (1988)
The Mirror and Other Strange Reflections (2002)
Eight Problems in Space: The Ensign De Ruyter Stories (2008)
The Adventures of Stately Homes and Sherman Horn (2008)
The Calabash of Coral Island and Other Early Stories (2008)

Forthcoming titles by Arthur Porges:

The Devil and Simon Flagg and Other Fantastic Tales
The Ruum and Other Science Fiction Stories
The Collected Essays of Arthur Porges
Spring, 1836: Selected Poems

The Miracle of the Bread
and Other Stories

Arthur Porges

Edited by Richard Simms

Richard Simms Publications

This paperback first edition published in 2008

Richard Simms Publications, Surrey, England

ISBN: 978-0-9556942-1-9

Copyright © 2008 The Estate of Arthur Porges

Introduction Copyright © 2008 Richard Simms

All rights reserved

No part of this book may be reproduced in any form, or by any means,
without prior permission in writing from the publisher.

With special thanks to Sue Wakefield, Cele Porges and Joel Hoffman.

For more information please visit The Arthur Porges Fan Site:

http://arthurporges.atwebpages.com

Contents

Introduction

Although Arthur Porges has been justifiably lauded for his many science fiction, fantasy and detective stories, this recognition has, regrettably, somewhat obscured the fact that he was a remarkably versatile writer. In terms of his short fiction as a whole, Arthur experimented and, in several cases excelled in numerous other genres.

The purpose of this collection is to showcase a variety of very different stories and, by so doing, illustrate Porges' abilities as a writer of quality short fiction, whatever the particular market he was writing for. At the same time, I have used this opportunity to bring to light several long forgotten tales that, I feel, definitely deserve another airing. In addition to this, I have included a number of what I consider to be quite excellent short stories—drawn from Arthur's original manuscripts—which are published here for the very first time.

In my previous book of Arthur's short stories, *The Calabash of Coral Island and Other Early Stories*, I assembled a selection of previously unpublished tales dating from the period before Porges' years of hard work and perseverance paid off when he sold his first story, "Modeled in Clay," in 1950. The stories covered a range of themes and genres, an editorial policy I have elected to continue with for this book. However, what you will find here are later stories—both published and unpublished and, of a generally much higher quality—that Arthur penned across a writing career lasting over fifty years. The earliest story in this collection dates from 1952 and the most recent was written in 2004.

A brief outline of the types of short fiction on display in this collection will give the reader an idea of Porges' wide thematic range. Within this book you will find stories about wild animals, juvenile fiction, war stories, offbeat fantasy, thrillers with elements of either mystery or science fiction—in one case both—and some stories that, as Arthur once put it, are just plain weird!

It may come as a surprise to those already familiar with Arthur's writings that a number of the tales included here are, in essence, very *human* in their subject matter. "Birthday in a Garden" is a coming-of-age story, whereas the poignant "The Only Survivor" is about an old man's terrible guilt. Others deal with loss, remembrance, what friendship really means; heady and emotive themes that are handled with remarkable sensitivity and compassion. All flowing from the pen of an author who is not supposed to be particularly gifted when it comes to characterization. Even Arthur himself recognized and freely admitted to this, but as you will see, in beautiful stories such as "The Crime" and "Weeping Willie," he was, at times, quite able to write about people with understanding and insight. When Arthur combines these qualities with his acclaimed gift for infusing stories with witty dialogue, humor and gritty realism, the reader will find much to appreciate here.

Before I go on to discuss the individual stories contained in this book, I should note that anyone impatient with facts, detail and analysis may wish to skip the rest of this introduction and get on with reading the stories! However, I do have some background material, personal observations and, I hope, various insights to offer those interested in such things.

Nine of the stories collected in this volume are previously unpublished. And we start off the book with one of these, the outstanding "Treed by Terror," written in the 1960s but unsold, despite the efforts of Arthur's agent, Scott Meredith Literary Agency. For sheer edge-of-your-seat excitement, the story is hard to beat. It's what a book reviewer might describe as "a tense thriller." And yet, this isn't a novel, it's a 3,200-word short story. An example, if any were needed, of how Porges managed to deftly squeeze so much detail into so few pages. On its most basic level, "Treed by Terror" is essentially about two people held at bay in the woods by a rabid dog. The story, on the surface, can be enjoyed as just that, but there is a lot more to it. It deals with the relationship between a teacher and one of his pupils, a disrespectful lad who the tutor is obliged to aid when the boy is faced with a dire, life-threatening situation. Without giving away too much, at its heart this is a story about respect. The teacher-pupil relationship is touched upon here to great effect; Porges cleverly leaves much unsaid. There is a good deal to admire about this story. The bristling tension, visceral realism and overlying sense of menace are neatly offset by the attention to the personalities of the characters, particularly that of the teacher Frank Osborn who, as the older of the two, is called upon to take charge of the situation. As a side note, it could be surmised that, in writing this tale, Arthur drew a little on his own experience as a college mathematics teacher—this is also true of the story "The Crime," which I will discuss later in this introduction.

"Weeping Willie" and "An Unlicensed Surgeon" are two very different stories that likewise went unpublished. The manuscript for the earlier of the two stories, "Weeping Willie," is dated December 18, 1960, when Porges was still—just—living at an address on Lockwood Avenue, Los Angeles. This was a couple of years after he retired from teaching to write full-time. Arthur was firing on all cylinders during this prolific period, managing to sell dozens of his stories to numerous magazines. "Weeping Willie," was, unjustly, one of the very few from this era that didn't sell. For it's a quite delightful story, a well structured piece that has something to say about childhood and cultural differences, while mixing it all up with some neat humor. Written much later, "An Unlicensed Surgeon" is, by contrast, a very grim adventure story about two brothers who, after surviving a plane crash, find themselves adrift on a life raft in the middle of the ocean. In typical fashion, Arthur creates a deadly predicament and conjures up a most unlikely and horrifying solution to a shocking situation. If you don't like sharks, look away.

The two stories that follow are equally effective but, once again, the subject matter couldn't be more different. Both stories found their way into the pages of the men's magazine *Escapade*. Apart from that fact, they have little in common. The first, "Reconstruction," published in 1956, provides a fascinating, authentic and compelling glimpse into the world of a sculptor. It's an artistic discipline that Arthur himself dabbled in; he once created some wire sculptures of outlandish anthropoid figures. His knowledge of the subject shines through in this well written, intriguing story and I think this aspect aptly illustrates that Porges' personal interests were not wholly focused in the scientific field. As is reflected in the diversity of stories assembled here, Arthur was interested in a wide range of subjects and read voraciously in all manner of fields as well as being a keen ornithologist and having a lifelong love of classical music. In his capacity as a writer of short fiction, he will justifiably be remembered most for his ingenuity in using little-known facts of science as plot devices and skillfully shaping a whole story structure around such authentic oddities. The central idea of "Reconstruction," concerned with creating—from scratch—a perfect sculptural facsimile of a human being based solely on footprints, is as clever as any used in his better known, more science-based stories. I am very pleased to reprint it here in this collection.

A few months later, Arthur was to sell a second story to *Escapade* magazine, the brilliant but unfairly ignored "Masterpiece," also from 1956. It is hard to describe the plot of this one without ruining the ending, but I will say that one of the strengths of this satirical tale, the setting of which is a downtown bar, is the acerbic, true-to-life dialogue. Porges also displays a gift for summing up the *look* of a character in just a few, well-chosen words, as in the opening paragraph:

The little man obviously was not sober, but neither was he drunk, although a single additional sip might have made him so. His eyes, soft and warm as melted caramel, shone with sincerity; and his fist, white, chubby, with immaculate nails, thumped the stained bar to emphasize his grievance.

Then there is the bartender, with his "small reptilian eyes" and the young blonde with a "flabby face" and fingers like "warm, greasy little sausages." Thus, in "Masterpiece" we enter into a seedy world of color, taste, texture and smell—not all of it pleasant! In this story an atmosphere of unease and anticipation is nurtured until the surprising, cynical and imaginative climax. Porges rated this story very highly indeed. On a personal note, I came across this piece quite late on in my own reading of Arthur's vast short fiction oeuvre. Suffice to say, it is the sign of a good author when they can still surprise you even after you've devoured an enormous amount of their output.

"Morning After," an unpublished gem written in the late fifties, also boasts a startling and unexpected ending. Like "Masterpiece," it cannot quite be classed as science fiction and this may have had something to do with the fact that it didn't sell. It is probable that the editors of the more genre-specific fiction magazines of the time didn't quite know what to make of it. And as a mere reader, one cannot guess where this story is going! A married couple—he a top TV writer and she his glamorous wife—who live on a secluded ranch in the Californian desert, wake up after a heavy night of "show-biz" partying. Their conversation is concerned with trivialities for the most part, as well as their growing confusion, which is central to the plot, as to the correct time of day. It is their everyday, commonplace concerns and good-natured bickering that not only endear the characters to the reader, but also help to create a sense of realism. As Larry Trent and his wife slowly wake up to the fact that something is wrong with the world, a disquieting mood begins to pervade the story. Read on ...

The next story, "Night of the Puppet," is another superb, vivid work that oddly didn't sell. It's a curious blend of detection and science fiction, a fusion of genres that is hardly unheard of, but in this instance it would seem the only explanation for the story being rejected. It follows the investigations of a Homicide Squad, led by Police Chief Kent Nolan, into a series of unexplained murders and holds the reader's attention from beginning to end. Arthur felt that "Night of the Puppet" contained one of his strongest ever story ideas and after its initial rejection, did not give up easily; he went on to write a slightly different version, which was duly submitted, again without success, to various periodicals. He even came up with an alternative title, "The Red Balloon." The differences between the story that appears here—in print for the first time—and the aforementioned revised version were minor; I adjudged the original treatment—and story title—marginally better.

From borderline science fiction we proceed to the black comedy and utter strangeness of the never-before-seen "Man's Best Friend," an unearthed and enigmatic tale that dates from 1960. I considered it good enough to publish, but it's the type of story you either love or hate. It concerns a quite objectionable, ill-tempered Irish terrier that torments its owner, the "man of the house," while adoring his wife. Poor Joe Caldwell, who Arthur bitingly describes as "small, pale and ineffectual," certainly has a rough time of it. There is a common belief that you are either a cat lover or a dog lover. Arthur was in the former group, so perhaps that goes some way towards explaining what inspired him to write this curious piece.

A few years ago I was undertaking some research at the British Library, delving into the history of short fiction in the—now defunct—London newspaper *The Evening News*. One of the many thousands of stories I came across in the pages of this once great treasure house of short fiction was Arthur Porges' "Secret Vice," published in the newspaper in 1962. I sent a copy of it to Arthur, thinking that he may never have seen the story in its published form, mindful of the fact that it was a British newspaper and Arthur lived in California. I was pleased when Arthur responded that he'd "quite forgotten" the story—although he had a copy in a scrapbook—and was delighted to reacquaint himself with a tale he'd written over forty years ago! It has never been reprinted, so I have taken the opportunity to include it here. Although the plot of "Secret Vice" bears no resemblance whatsoever to "Man's Best Friend," the two stories sit neatly alongside each other in that both are dark, comic fantasies.

"The Drum Major" originally sneaked its way into the pages of *Alfred Hitchcock's Mystery Magazine* in 1962. It has been reprinted in book form prior to its appearance here and deservedly so. One wouldn't describe it as a fantasy exactly, although the entire narrative is made up of an imaginative dream sequence, engendering an obvious feeling of unreality. "The Drum Major" is a chilling story that embodies much that is good about Arthur's more outré fiction; a sense of poetry, the use of evocative imagery, an unsettling glimpse into a tortured mind. Arthur once told me that this story was partly inspired by his reading of the short fiction of Rudyard Kipling. He went on to say that he felt the recurring motif of the marshal drums, so much like heartbeats, was right for the story; in short, a mood piece.

In terms of its overall tone, "The Crime" is a disquieting, haunting, almost painfully honest tale, expertly handled as regards to its measured approach and careful understatement. Arthur certainly utilized his own experience here, with the central character, Joe Polanski, being, like the author, a college mathematics teacher from Illinois. "The Crime" appeared in print back in 1965; ironically in an obscure pin-up magazine called *Romper*. The publication of this fine story in such a racy—though tame by today's standards—periodical may have been down to the sexual undercurrent that pervades this masterful work. But that aside, it deserved a better, shall we say, more respectable, outlet. Porges concurred with this sentiment, going so far as to remark that he believed "The Crime" to be his best "literary" story, considering it worthy of inclusion in *Harper's* or *The Atlantic*.

The same might be said of the following two stories in this collection. In the fascinating and whimsical "A Letter from Réjane," Arthur shows his love and appreciation of the theatre. Subtly understated and told with a skillful economy of words, it is an example of Porges' more reflective work. These qualities are also in evidence in "Birthday in a Garden," a story about growing up and paternal love; the difficulty in facing up to the fact of having to let someone go, no matter the heartbreak caused by their departure. Porges is noted for writing stories that revolve around a clever plot-device; one could argue that the characters, in much of his fiction, are subsidiary. But in "Birthday in a Garden," the characters *are* the story and it is none the worse for that. One can only wonder why neither of these two stories, which incidentally date from the 1960s, saw publication.

Arthur had a lifelong interest in natural history and was addicted to reading nature stories as a young man. Surprisingly, he only ever sold two of his own stories about wild animals; "The Odyssey of

Epeira" and "The Black Tyrant" were published in *Boys' Life* magazine in 1952 and 1955 respectively. The former title has an interesting publishing history. The editor of *Boys' Life*, on accepting the story, felt that Arthur's title was too esoteric for kids and changed it to "Eight Legged Monster"—with, it must be said, the author's blessing. However, for its inclusion here, the first time it has been reprinted anywhere else, I have chosen to reinstate the original name which, I feel, is superior. The story itself, a chronicle of the adventures of a garden spider, is a perfect example of how Porges was able to imbue so many of his tales with authentic detail. It is, perhaps, this quality that makes the story come alive in the mind of the reader. Amusingly, Arthur may have been compelled to write "The Odyssey of Epeira" by his genuine fondness for spiders. Writing in an article published in the late 1980s, he admitted he was loath to remove any cobwebs from his house; beautiful designs that Porges appreciated had been painstakingly constructed! On a more academic note, this story, in common with the long-unpublished "The Soulless Ones: Vespa"— now available in the volume *The Calabash of Coral Island and Other Early Stories* (2008)—was inspired by essays contained in the English edition of Fabre's *Souvenirs Entomologiques*.

"The Black Tyrant," the second of the *Boys' Life* stories, reads like a dream. Infused with realism, it's another wildlife story, this time concerned with the exploits of a raven. It has everything; pace, authenticity, atmosphere and excitement, as exemplified in the following passage:

> Rark hopped reluctantly off the fish, regarding the intruder with warning haughtiness. Was he, Rark, master of the air for miles around, whom even the terrible falcons of Chalk Ledge dared not molest in flight, to be robbed of his prize by a sneaking red rascal? He danced about angrily with half-opened wings, glancing down his wicked beak at the advancing fox.

An account of the raven's confrontation with a snowy owl, which appears later in the tale, is likewise brilliantly executed. "The Black Tyrant" is certainly an accomplished work, but to temper all this richly deserved high praise, it is worth pointing out that the inspiration for this story no doubt owed something to the writings of Henry Williamson and Ernest Thompson Seton, two of Arthur's favorite authors.

It is a cause for regret that Porges produced no other nature yarns in the years to follow—aside from "By a Fluke" (1955), a science fiction story that involves, would you believe, a study of the life cycle of a parasitic flatworm! He did, however, utilize his knowledge of ornithology in later stories such as "Circle in the Dust" (1960), "Movie Show" (1999) and "The Fiery Patriot" (1965), the latter a World War Two story; the first in an interconnected series of adventures which I have assembled for this book.

There were five stories in the series—the first four of which ran in *Argosy* magazine from 1965 through 1966—chronicling the escapades of one David Selby, a young Private—later promoted to the rank of Lieutenant—in the U.S. Army. Selby's ingenuity is called upon in each story to foil the Nazis; the setting for all but one entry in the series is Occupied France. The individual stories in this thrilling sequence of wartime escapades follow the same basic pattern; the military problem, which has confounded all the experts, is explained to Selby, who then has to come up with a solution. Thus in "Last Gasp," Selby's imagination and scientific knowledge is used to help a British bomb-disposal unit safely disable an unexploded German bomb that has been booby-trapped with diabolical cleverness. In "The Room," Selby must set fire to a chamber full of important documents from outside, through a permanently closed window—while leaving no trace of his method! My personal favorite in the series is "Dressed to Kill," where he faces his toughest challenge yet: his job is to enter, under cover, a heavily guarded German plant and sabotage a vital piece of machinery that produces electronic components for a new torpedo to be used against allied submarines.

Those familiar with one of Porges' other series characters, Ensign De Ruyter—whose exploits are collected in the book *Eight Problems in Space*, published by The Battered Silicon Dispatch Box in 2008—will recognize a similarity between the two men. Like De Ruyter, Selby is a young, gifted, military genius, liked and respected by his superiors and noted for his ingenuity and puzzle-solving ability. And in common with the sleuths that feature in a number of Arthur's detective stories, it is obscure facts of science that Selby employs to triumph in seemingly impossible circumstances.

The Selby stories found a suitable home in *Argosy*, which, at the time, advertised itself as "The No. 1 Men's Service Magazine." Strange then, that the last entry in the series, "Murder of a Priest," was published instead in *Ellery Queen's Mystery Magazine* in 1967.

Another WWII story Porges wrote was "Stalemate." It was printed in *Argosy* magazine in 1961, a few years prior to the Selby series. A study in suspense, this is a tightly written and tense piece, which Arthur aptly described as "too clever by half." Set in the last days of the war, as the Allied forces battle their way into Germany, it tells of a bizarre incident that occurs between two American soldiers and a fanatical Nazi sniper. Arthur drew on his own wartime experience as an artillery instructor to augment this tale with some authenticity. The big "one-o-fives" mentioned in the story are a reference to the 105 Howitzer guns that Porges recalled from his days of teaching gunnery mathematics in the U.S. Army.

For the next story we move forward in time over thirty years. "The Only Survivor" was published in *Ellery Queen's Mystery Magazine* in 1994, the editor describing it as "a wonderfully compressed piece of fiction." In less than a thousand words, Porges tells the story of a dying man's confession to a priest which is focused on his remorse over an incident that occurred in the aftermath of a battle that took place over sixty years ago. The narrator of the tale relates, in vivid detail, what happened during the Strelsau massacre— Porges does not give the name of the country or the date—of which he was the lone survivor. An intriguing yarn that Arthur imbued with a subtle poignancy, "The Only Survivor" did not in fact appear in the author's preferred form. On hearing that his story was accepted for publication, Porges decided, on reflection, to rewrite the story and duly sent it off to Janet Hutchings, the editor of *EQMM*, urging her to use his improved version instead of the original. Unfortunately this did not happen, much to his disappointment. The reworked manuscript came into my possession after Arthur passed away in 2006 and I have decided to publish it here. The differences between the two treatments are fairly subtle; some names and minor details have been changed but the plot remains untouched. Those who own the May 1994 issue of *Ellery Queen's Mystery Magazine* can judge for themselves which version is better.

"The Most Dangerous Animal in the World" was also published late on in his career. As with the previous story, Porges wrote several versions of this tale. His original treatment dates from a period back in the 1950s when he was living a semi-beachcombing existence in his rose-covered house at Laguna Beach in Southern California. It didn't sell and nor did a much later revision, now in the form of a duologue, which in my opinion would have made a great short play for radio. Several decades were to pass before Arthur finally hit upon a winning formula—augmented with some necessary updating for a modern audience—in 1999 and sold the story to the long-running *Cricket* magazine, a monthly publication aimed at readers aged 9 to 14. The story's intrinsic sense of wonder and educational content made its eventual placement in *Cricket* appropriate, although it can be enjoyed by readers of all ages. One cannot say too much about the story itself without spoiling it for the reader. It takes the form of a reminiscence, to a time long ago when a group of children pay a visit to an eccentric, but widely traveled and knowledgeable, old man who challenges his young guests to answer the question overt in the title of the story.

The final piece in this volume is another look back into the distant past. Written in 2004, "The Miracle of the Bread" is one of the last stories Porges ever wrote. It takes the form of a monologue, with the narrator of the story giving us a moving account of an extraordinary event from his childhood. It is Christmas Eve in 1925 and a ten-year-old boy's mother is seriously ill from an infection. There were no antibiotics back then to strengthen her fragile hold on life; what is needed is a miracle. As the story unfolds, we are drawn more and more into the child's desperate plight to save his mother. "The Miracle of the Bread" contains some fascinating period detail, no doubt inspired, at least in part, by Arthur's own experience of growing up in a lower middle class neighborhood of Chicago. I was unaware of the existence of this story until a few months after Arthur died; as a result of this I can only guess at what inspired him to write it. Arthur's mother died of an illness when he was very young; a fact that leads me to believe that this, very touching, tale was written from the heart.

A fitting conclusion, I think, to a collection of short stories that are very close to my heart. For it should be obvious from this extensive commentary that my desire to publish these stories stems from a deep appreciation of them. It has been an honor to compile this volume of Arthur Porges' short fiction and I hope all who read this book find much to enjoy here.

Richard Simms
Surrey, England
July, 2008

Treed by Terror

Frank Osborn was too tired for a man of thirty-two, and the shell fragments in his right leg were hurting again, as if each little burr of metal was red-hot. Almost four o'clock, and sixty-odd chemistry papers to grade this evening. There was no longer the same pleasure in teaching. These kids weren't like the ones he'd known a few years back. You'd think that here, in a small community, with good hunting and fishing, some of the old virtues would still prevail. But no; too many of the boys were big, husky louts with no respect for learning; and a lot of the others were even worse: pasty-faced, slick punks, who acted as if they were on dope, or sniffing glue.

Osborn knew that his own standards had slipped, too. Instead of trying to pound some theory into the class, he was inclined to settle for spectacular demonstrations, like the one today, with silvery metal sputtering into violet flame. Keep the animals diverted; otherwise, one of these days, he might lose control and clout some overgrown wise guy. That would tear it; he'd be out on his ear. Nowadays, for a hundred-and-forty-pound man to sock a boy who outweighed him was aggravated assault.

He sighed, pausing at the fork in the road. The path into the woods was tempting, and would save him a mile of the hike home. His bad leg needed that break tonight; actually, he should have taken the car. But there were wild dogs on the loose in those inviting green thickets.

Most of them were probably just small mongrels, still respectful of man, but lately at least two new brutes had joined the others. One was a huge Doberman; the second dog was an Alsatian, almost as big. Last week they had treed a man, keeping him aloft in a sweat of fear until driven off by the approach of an armed party. One of the dogs may have been nicked by a bullet; nobody was sure. Then, only last night, one of the two had killed a cow, first mangling the watchdog, a spunky terrier, completely outmatched. Osborn decided he was in no mood to tangle with such killers.

So he limped on, favoring the weak leg, and thinking of the stack of papers to be graded at home before he could really settle down with a stiff drink and a detective story. And there was the matter of the potassium, too. One of the kids had stolen the little vial of shiny metal. Almost certainly he knew who it was. But just try accusing anybody without complete evidence. Why didn't the boy take just a sliver? In Osborn's day he and his friends had often snitched things for home experimentation: acid, and potassium nitrate to make fuses; but nobody carried off the whole damn supply at once.

He was considering the problem of reordering, when he heard the shout, so faint but urgent. Somebody was calling for help, and the voice was shrill with fear.

Osborn muttered a curse. Another damned tenderfoot lost in the woods. They never learned to sit tight and make a little smoke. Instead the idiots ran wild, usually in a circle, until they collapsed from exhaustion. Every now and then one even died of fear—with town never more than ten miles away, too.

For a moment he debated getting on home, and calling the sheriff. Then he shook his head in annoyance. It would be dark in two hours or less. The guy sounded real scared. Maybe he'd better go after him right now; the sheriff might be off at the other end of the county. Angry at the world, Osborn retraced his steps back to the fork in the road, and plunged into the woods, heading towards the anguished voice, now calling without pause, and quavering with terror.

There was something familiar about the sound of it; Osborn broke into a gimpy run, wondering what could cause such fear. He broke through into a small clearing, and found out. The boy was clinging to the trunk of a tree, while just below, making one savage leap after another, was a great bluish Doberman. It was a poor choice the kid had made, Osborn thought immediately. There was no branch at all within reach, and Field was hugging the trunk barely above the dog's clashing teeth. One foot seemed to be on a stub or bulge, but otherwise the boy had no support worth a hang.

At the sight of the man, he began to sob.

"Help me!" he begged. "Mr. Osborn, help me. I can't hold on any more."

The Doberman stopped his jumping, and turned a great, cruel head towards Osborn. Then, in a sudden irrational frenzy, he circled the tree, snapping at the earth, dead leaves, and even his own flanks, uttering low, mournful howls.

Osborn felt his blood thicken to an icy jelly. Every man has a secret fear, and this was his. He knew all about rabies. It was the worst death in the world, painful and degrading to the last degree. There was the Pasteur treatment, to be sure, but sometimes the cure was almost as bad as the disease, and left a person with a ruined nervous system, like a victim of muscular dystrophy or multiple sclerosis.

"Mr. Osborn," the boy whimpered again. "Please, Mr. Osborn, help me!"

"Hang on, Dave," Osborn shouted. "You gotta hang on." What the hell did the boy expect him to do—fight the dog barehanded? He'd hate to tackle the beast with a club, even if the Doberman wasn't rabid. But it was, definitely. Got nipped by a hydrophobic skunk, or maybe a coyote; there were always a few around. Even rabid bats, they said.

At the sound of his voice, the dog stopped those mad circlings, and began to sidle his way. That wouldn't do at all. Osborn looked around for a good tree, found one with low branches, and forgetting his game leg, went up fast. But the Doberman had lost interest in him, and returned to the boy. Possibly Field's terror was the lure; a dog could smell deep fear.

"Help!" Osborn roared, using the full power of his lungs. "Help—mad dog out here!" It was just possible somebody back at the road might hear him. But not too probable; traffic was very light at this time of the day, with the consolidated school closed.

"Why the hell are you out here?" he demanded in exasperation. "You're supposed to take the bus."

"I had some traps set," the boy gulped.

"I'll bet you did," Osborn snapped. "Against the law, too." To himself he added: Wouldn't put it past that punk to torture anything he catches. I oughta leave him for the dog! But he knew that was impossible.

"I can't hold on!" Field whimpered.

"Try to get higher on the trunk—up to a branch."

"I can't, Mr. Osborn—I can't. Help me, please."

The man began to search his pockets. Nothing much; not even a knife. Just a couple of chocolate bars. But they gave him an idea.

"Listen," he yelled. "I'll throw down some food. If he comes for it, you drop down and run like hell for that big tree with the low branches."

"I can't," the boy sobbed. "He'll catch me. I'm afraid."

"He'll be eating; I'll keep him busy. It'll only take you a few seconds." He broke one of the bars into thirds, and called to the Doberman. "Here, boy—eats! Come and get it."

The dog seemed to be over his fit of madness; his ears pricked up. Osborn saw that he was gaunt to the point of emaciation.

"Here, boy!" he cried, and tossed the chocolate near the foot of his own tree.

The Doberman saw it fall, hesitated, then loped over.

"Now, run, Field—run, you idiot!" Osborn cried. But the boy held fast, his body shaking to his sobs.

"I can't; I'll never make it. I can't; oh, my God!"

At the sound of his voice, the great hound snarled again. He left Osborn and went back to the other tree. He looked up at the boy, growling, and began a new series of leaps. Field's cries began to sound hysterical, and Osborn feared he would drop right into the animal's jaws. Why couldn't the punk have some courage? A sneaky, insolent type right from the start. Surely, he was the one—

"Field!" Osborn called urgently. "Did you take that potassium? Answer me!"

The accusation, oddly enough, seemed to steady the boy; maybe he was used to such challenges.

"I ain't got your old potassium," he said.

"Don't lie," Osborn snapped. "Tell me the truth. Maybe it can help us." Even as he thought about it, his hope rose. Just drop a fragment of that metal in the dog's mouth, or better, get him to swallow it, and the Doberman would forget about them in a hurry. A nasty thing to do to a dumb animal, but there wasn't much choice.

"I took it," the boy said, "but I ain't got it now."

"Oh, great!" Osborn said in disgust. "Where is it, then?"

"I dropped it in a puddle back there—you know, to make it explode."

"Well, that kills one idea," the man said. "The only one, I'm afraid." He reflected for a moment. Without the potassium, what was left? There was still fire of some sort. With a good torch, there might be an angle. If he jabbed it into the dog's throat good and hard, the shock and possibly a bad burn on the sensitive parts could drive the Doberman away, at least for a few minutes, which was all the time they'd need to get clear of the trap.

Osborn searched his pockets again; there should be a packet of paper matches in one of them. He found one, opened it, and gave a grunt of annoyance. Just three matches left; not much of a margin; still, they should be enough. Now how to make a torch.

Cautiously he reached up into the tree, and tore away a thin branch. He stripped off the leaves, and hefted the thing. It was about a yard long; more like a whip than a torch, he thought. Certainly no good as it was.

He thought for a moment, then in a gingerly way, peeled off his shirt. Hastily he tore it into strips, which he then wrapped around the tip of the branch, tying them in place.

"Help me!" the boy shrieked. "My arms are getting dead."

"Pretty soon," Osborn told him soothingly.

Locking his thighs tightly to the tree, torch hugged under his left arm, he struck a match and brought it to the mass of cloth. But before it even touched, a vagrant puff of air blew out the tiny flame.

"Brother!" Osborn groaned. "One gone for nothing."

He tipped the torch so that the end was nearer his right hand, and tried again, nursing the small flame. This time he got it to the cloth, but to his dismay the material only bubbled and melted.

For a moment he watched in surprise; then his eyes narrowed, and he swore, softly but with venom, between clenched teeth. Of course! The shirt was one of those damned plastic synthetic things, fireproof, waterproof, and generally clammy. A great torch that would make!

Resisting an impulse to drop the whole mess to the ground, he jammed the branch into a fork over his head, and took a fresh look at the situation.

Luckily the great hound was reasonably quiet just now, lying under Field's tree, and merely growling occasionally as the boy tried to ease his cramped limbs.

"What about the torch you were making?" he demanded, and the Doberman stood up, snarling.

"Shut up!" Osborn hissed. "If you talk, he'll start jumping again."

"I can't hold on much longer," the boy said. "You gotta do something."

"Shut up, I said; let me think."

There was still his undershirt; that was cotton, and should burn fairly well. But there was a problem, anyhow—only one match left, and that wasn't likely to be enough. If there was something he could put on the cloth to make it really flare up … gasoline, or ether … He stiffened suddenly.

"Field! Was there any kerosene left in that potassium vial?"

"Kerosene? Maybe—gee, I don't know."

"Well, think, damn it. Where did you leave the vial after you used the potassium?"

"It should be over there, just past the big bush. That's where I was when the dog chased me."

Osborn estimated the distance: about a hundred yards; no more. And, luckily, in the direction away from Field's tree—and the Doberman. It was worth a try.

He took out the rest of the chocolate bar, picked a good spot past the dog, and yelled: "Here, boy! Food!"

Again the animal responded, getting to his feet expectantly. Osborn balanced the candy in the palm of his hand, aimed—and froze. It was something he just couldn't help. The thought of actually dropping to the ground while hoping the dog would be occupied with the chocolate, no longer seemed attractive, or even bearable. How could he get away with it, and with a bum leg? Risk having that huge brute, undoubtedly mad, savage him? The tiniest nip, the slightest break in the skin, meant the whole Pasteur treatment, with all its dangers. Nobody could expect him to try it.

The Doberman came trotting up now; that made it worse; for he was too close. The gaunt animal, foam at his jaws, glared up at Osborn, and rumbled deep in his throat. The man felt that the luminous yellow eyes, full of insensate rage, were reading his mind; that the dog suspected his plan. Why did it have to be such a big animal? They said that whatever a man feared most always came to him sooner or later. Osborn closed his eyes, and fought dizziness briefly. Field was whimpering again. There simply wasn't any choice.

Aiming again with great care, he flipped the bit of candy well past the boy's tree. It was a good stroke, and the dog, seeing the chocolate drop, ran over. The second he started, Osborn scrambled down, and made his own foray, racing towards the bush.

He made it quite fast, in spite of the weak leg, and spotted the vial immediately. It was overturned and quite empty. All for nothing, was his first thought, but there was no time for a second. The Doberman, having gobbled the bit of candy, had followed him, and now blocked the way to his tree.

Osborn backed off, his eyes searching desperately for a new, better perch. They found one, but none too close. The dog increased his pace, growling softly. Obviously he was about to charge, so Osborn ran for it. Even as he hobbled over the rough ground, he saw clearly in his imagination the poisonous white teeth tearing first at his ankles, then higher up, where a bite was even more dangerous. He didn't seem to think about being killed, even though that was highly probable; there was overriding horror just in the aftermath of those rabid snaps.

"Run, Mr. Osborn—run!" Field was yelling, his voice full of horror. "He's after you!"

The man knew better than to look back. On reaching the chosen tree, he scrambled up like a squirrel, never quite realizing how he made it. There was just the feel of his nails on bark, the stabs of anguish in his flailing leg, and the immense relief of finding himself safe on the big branch. Only then, when he saw the blobs of foam on his right heel, did he come close to collapse.

"I'm slipping!" the boy gasped. "My arms are all numb." He clawed frantically for a better hold.

"There's a knob or something just over your left hand," Osborn told him. "You can't see it, but it's there. It's a better grip."

The boy inched his fingers up, found the burl, and dug in with his nails. That gave him a chance to adjust his right arm. Osborn saw with relief that Field was safe for another little while. He needed the time to figure a new angle. He really could use one: the torch across the clearing in another tree, and a single match left.

"You got any matches?" he called.

"Matches?" the boy repeated in a dull voice. "No. But I got a lighter," he added, with more animation.

"Any fluid in it?"

"I dunno; I guess so."

"Look at it and see," Osborn snapped. A lot of help he was getting!

Gingerly, holding on with his left hand over the burl, the boy dipped into a pocket. He shook the lighter.

"It's pretty full, I think."

That's it, Osborn thought. With fluid I can fix up a good torch. "Toss it as near to me as you can," he ordered Field.

The boy made an excellent throw, the lighter falling about five feet from Osborn's tree. Immediately the dog ran to it, apparently hoping for more food. For a moment Osborn thought the crazed brute was going to carry it off in his jaws, but after a couple of sniffs, he let it lie there. A mournful wail came from his throat; he bit at his flanks, splattering them with froth.

Osborn took out the other chocolate bar. This had to be a double play. Get to the lighter, and then back to the torch, still to be remade with cotton.

Once more he got the dog's attention by calling to him, and this time tossed the whole bar, scheming to keep him busy a few seconds longer. When the Doberman went for the food, Osborn dropped down, grabbed the lighter, and was back at the other tree before the animal finished eating.

Hurriedly the man pulled off his undershirt, shivering in the cool air, and wrapped it sloppily over the cloth already in place.

"Here, boy!" he called, but the dog wasn't interested. Instead, he was snarling beneath the boy again, and Field was beginning to slide. If the Doberman decided to jump, and put his heart into it, he would surely get a grip, now. And with a hundred-plus pounds of rabid beast fastened to him, the boy would soon be dragged down and mangled. Osborn knew he had to work fast.

He fished some coins from his pocket, and hurled them at the dog, which growled as one struck his face. But he still glared up at Field, and crouched to spring.

"Hey!" Osborn roared, using his full non-com voice. "Get away! Garn—shoo!"

The great hound turned those opalescent eyes towards him, lips wrinkled malignantly. Osborn slipped off a shoe. "Scat!" he shouted, throwing the heavy oxford right at the animal's head. It struck a hind leg, but that was enough. The dog went wild with fury, running to the base of Osborn's tree, and leaping at least eight inches higher than before. Startled, the man snatched his lower foot, now protected only by a sock, to a safer level, and the clashing jaws, dripping saliva, just missed his heel.

Osborn, his heart pounding with something close to panic, hugged the tree. Then he saw that Field had slid down almost to the ground, and there was no time for fear.

Shouting at the dog, to keep his attention, the man grabbed the torch, and was about to pour lighter fluid over it, when a new idea hit home. The flaming wad of cotton might work, but it was by no means certain. A minor burn around the mouth could make the dog wilder without driving him off. But there was a better way.

He poured a few drops on the cloth; just enough to make a wet patch the size of a quarter. Then he began to taunt the Doberman, growling, meowing, and jeering, until the huge hound was frantic to get at him.

When the panting dog crouched once more to jump, Osborn leaned far down, holding on with his left hand, and poured lighter fluid all over the animal's back.

For a moment the Doberman flattened himself to the ground suspicious of the sudden moisture. Osborn flicked the lighter, knowing the damp wick would burn briefly, and lit the end of his torch. Then, as the dog made another desperate leap, the man touched the burning torch to the animal's back. Instantly the dog was on fire, an area of almost a square foot flickering with blue flames on shoulders and sides.

There was a terrible squall of agony from the Doberman. He spun in a circle, yelping, rolled about in a paroxysm of fear, and then ran off into the woods. The shrill sounds faded away in the distance. Osborn didn't feel proud. He hated to do such a thing to a dumb brute, especially when it was already doomed to a miserable death by disease. But it would be dark soon, and Field was done for, so what choice did he have?

Very stiffly, his leg throbbing, he climbed down. The boy was just lying there, quivering in a state of near hysteria.

"Come on," Osborn said gruffly. "No time for that. He may be back; the burn isn't bad enough to disable him much. Besides there could be more of the pack around."

In the deepening twilight he led the way back to the road.

"Gonna tell the principal—about the potassium, I mean?" Field quavered.

"No. But next time you steal chemicals, don't be such a damned hog."

"What if we didn't have that lighter fluid?"

"Then I'd have had the pleasant choice of watching you torn apart, or tackling that dog barehanded. And there wasn't even a good

30

rock around, in case you didn't notice. What would I have done? Don't ask me. Who the hell can fight a mad dog that size barehanded?"

The boy was silent, and Osborn suddenly remembered the stack of papers, on which were scribbled formulas for compounds unknown to the best chemists in the world. He groaned.

"Well, *I* know what you'd have done," Field said. "You'd have taken that dog on, no matter what."

There was a new note of respect in the boy's voice, and Osborn felt more cheerful. The bad leg and the papers didn't seem to matter greatly.

They reached the fork in the road.

"See you tomorrow, Dave."

"Yes, sir," the boy replied, in an unusually subdued voice.

Weeping Willie

"Why do the other kids call Bill 'Weeping Willie'?" Charles demanded, his voice accusing. "That's no name for a nine-year-old boy, I must say. Especially mine. I just passed some little imp out there, all dirt and freckles, and he said to one of his friends: "Hey, there goes Weeping Willie's dad." Since when did I acquire that unpleasant title?"

Colette's eyes, ordinarily sea-blue like the waters of her native Normandy, darkened. Then she smiled.

"It's nothing to worry about, *cheri*. Do not concern yourself over Bill. They call him that because he cries easily. Not so much when he is hurt, mind you, but when he is angry or frustrated. Then the big tears come—like rivers they roll down his cheeks. Never have I seen so much water flow from so small a child."

"The devil you say!" Charles snapped, his face grim under the bushy brows. "My son acting like a sissy. How long has this been going on?"

"He has always been one to cry for the least thing," his wife said placidly. "You have been away too much by day to notice. At night, in the house, with just the three of us, it is different, naturally. But don't forget he is half French. In my country, a man weeps as easily as a woman. It does not make him less a man, you comprehend. But you Americans—you forbid the boys to cry. That is not good. If a boy

32

cannot cry, he must explode. And then—pouf—" she made a typically Gallic gesture with her slim hands—"the gangs, the senseless violence; and then somebody is dead."

"You may be right about that," Charles said, "but we live in America, not France; and in this country a boy who cries like a girl will be left out of everything. He won't have a friend in the neighborhood. Why, that could ruin a kid's future. I'll have to talk to Bill and straighten him out. Weeping Willie!" he snorted. "No son of mine is ever going to be called that, not if I can help it."

"It would be unwise to say anything to him," Colette warned. "You may build a barrier of separation that way. The tears mean nothing. My father, too, cried over small matters. Many times, during the Occupation, he and my mother wept in each other's arms. But still he went on working for the Resistance. No doubt he cried when he shot Colonel Diekmann at Gestapo Headquarters—the one who hanged a dozen hostages—but the Nazi was just as dead as if *mon père* had laughed instead."

"That may be all right in France," Charles persisted stubbornly, "but it won't do here. You can't expect the kids Bill plays with to understand the French temperament. All they know is that a boy is either chicken or he's not. And if he's chicken, they'll hound him to death out of here. No, Colette, I'll have to settle this with Bill right now. He's out there someplace, with the others. Don't look so stricken; I won't hurt the boy. I promise to be very tactful."

He took a step towards the door, but his wife, moving with the speed and grace of a panther, barred the way. Her little, heart-shaped face was alight with some inner glow of anticipation.

"No!" she cried. "Not now, Charles. Here, by the window. Watch—and listen; but do not be seen. It commences. Your son is about to cry."

He stared at her. Then the babble of young voices outside the study window drew his attention. Colette made a fierce, imperious little gesture towards the curtains. He had almost forgotten this tigress-side of his wife; but obediently moved to a position that gave him a good view of the yard. There was a ragged circle of youngsters out there, forming an impromptu arena of the sort that must have appeared regularly in various American towns since 1776. Inside that living ring, Charles saw his son Bill, a small, sturdy figure, oddly pale compared to the tanned faces on all sides. Bill was the blond type that burned and peeled repeatedly in the California sun, but never darkened. Like Colette, Charles thought briefly, before returning his entire concentration to the essential drama before him.

Facing Bill in the center of the circle was another boy, perhaps two years older. He was a lanky redhead, with a narrow, sullen face. It suggested slyness rather than courage, until you noticed the jaw, disproportionately large and craggy. Charles knew the type, and felt a sudden thrill of memory, recalling a summer thirty years earlier, in Ohio. Yes, this was the authentic genus bully. Not the traditional coward of the cheap juvenile novels, who tormented younger children and fled from the hero, but the boy from a bad home, full of wild courage, and warped by love of violence.

Charles watched the tension mounting, fascinated and appalled by the spectacle. Why, the little brute had four inches and ten pounds on Bill. Already his son was crying; a veritable stream of tears was pouring from each eye. Never had he seen such profuse weeping. This was no mere sobbing, but more like a cataract.

Charles started to turn away. "I'd better stop that in a hurry," he muttered. "They're egging Bill into a nasty beating. It's not fair; the other kid's much too big and tough. And Bill's scared to death. My God, look at him bawl."

Once again Colette barred his path. Her fingers dug into his heavy shoulders; her eyes were now more like stormy seas in their yellow opalescence.

"Stay here!" she hissed. "Do not meddle now. Just watch. You were concerned about your son's tears. See how he cries. Watch and learn."

"Weeping Willie!" one of the spectators yelled; and others took up the chorus. "Weeping Willie! Give it to ol' Red, Willie!"

"Lookit 'im cry," the older boy jeered. "I hate to hit the little baby. Let 'im run home to mommy."

The circle contracted, forcing the two children closer together. Outside some frustrated little girls hopped and screamed excitedly, unable to see. The bully sprang forward, light on his feet, a veteran of many fights. With an open hand he contemptuously shoved hard at Bill's chest. The smaller boy staggered, almost falling. The crowd yelled. The redhead danced in again. This time he swung a fist, knotty and freckled. It landed squarely on Bill's eye.

"There's something to bawl about!" the lanky boy grinned.

"Out of my way!" Charles said to Colette. "What kind of mother are you to stand there and let them do a thing like this to your son?"

"*Non, non,*" Colette begged, subsiding, in her agitation, into a stream of French. "*Reste ici, Charles. Regardez*—watch. It's always like this. Bill, he does not want to fight. He is an artist, like my *grandpère*. He knows how foolish it all is. But do not fear. *Bien!* Now you will see."

And truly Charles did see, and the sight made him gulp with disbelief. For Bill, weeping great tears still, suddenly became a windmill of flying fists. Completely indifferent now to the punishing blows of the redhead, he closed in like some irresistible robot. Charles realized abruptly that although his son would never be tall, there was a chunky solidity about him that spoke of hidden power. The small shoulders were oddly heavy and thrusting, like Charles' own; the young wrists thick with muscle. Under the merciless flailing of Bill's knuckles, the lanky redhead gave ground. Then he crumpled to the earth, with Bill on top of him, pounding away. The ring contracted to a heaving knot of boys, and Charles heard the swelling chorus of young voices, shrill with exultation.

"Atta boy, Weeping Willie! He did it! Red's through! Ya-a-a-y!" One triumphant shriek soared above the others. To Charles' surprise, it came from a grubby little blonde girl hopelessly trying to pierce the barrier of boys.

Colette was tugging at his sleeve. "*Voila!* It is over. Move away before one of them sees you."

"He cries," Charles said. "But he fights—Lord, how he fights. Like a little demon."

"Exactly. That is my point. Always he cries, and does not wish to battle. But he always wins. This red one is the last."

"The last?"

"Truly. For miles around there is nobody left to challenge our son. His little friends, they are foolish, and maybe a tiny bit cruel, too; they make him fight for their honor. But they are only babies; and it is the custom here. Now he has won over all, and they will not ask again. He is their leader until they grow a little and recognize the foolishness they have done."

"Then that name, Weeping Willie—it's just a nickname, an honorable one; they really like him."

"But of course. He is their hero. None of them would have dared to face the red boy. It is like the man we called 'Mademoiselle', during the Occupation. A skinny little thing with a girl's soft eyes and gentleness. But in battle, he was worth a dozen big hairy farmers. Be wise, Charles, and say nothing to our boy about this name. He will think that you do not comprehend—that you doubt his courage."

"I won't say a word," Charles said, grinning hugely. He kissed Colette. "After what Bill did to that big redhead, I'd be afraid to!"

An Unlicensed Surgeon

"They actually seem to envy us," Chris Banfield said to his brother. "The damned fools!" he added bitterly.

He looked around the grill with a stare that was provocatively insolent. His blue eyes, like the muzzles of two loaded pistols in their chilly menace, made most other gazes fall. Only some of the women met the challenge directly, intrigued by his hard maleness and gargoyle face, all seams, ridges and red scar tissue.

"Why not?" Larry asked in a sardonic voice. "We survived the worst plane crash in years and collected almost half a million dollars to boot. The lucky Banfield boys," he reminded Chris, smiling mirthlessly. "They forget about Mark, Wally, and Tim—just married, too—at the bottom of the sea."

"Ah!" Chris said. "Some of these clowns would gladly sell three brothers for half that dough—and maybe throw in a sister, too."

Their eyes met knowingly, and in a heartbeat they were back in time eighteen months, in distance a thousand miles …

Two men in a rubber raft, incongruously gay in fluorescent yellow, alone on the water under a pitiless sun that seemed hot enough to melt lead. Four hundred fathoms below them was the shattered plane, a tomb for sixty-eight people, including three of the five Banfield brothers.

Two men, weak, dehydrated; situation almost hopeless; Chris with his face a mass of oozing blisters, and Larry, the exposed bone of his left arm chalk-white against the purple of gangrenous flesh.

There was a third actor in the tragedy—a huge, grey-white shark tirelessly circling the raft, their constant companion for the last ten days. Grimly humorous, they had named it Jack the Ripper.

"Dad always claimed Banfields lived fast and died hard," Larry said, "and with this lovely compound fracture I'm about to prove the second half—in spades. It hurts—and smells to high heaven."

"Don't say that," Chris mumbled through fire-seared lips. "You're still far from dead." He studied Larry's arm. "If I can take that off, you'll have a fighting chance. Remember Uncle Mike at Tarawa. They wrote him off with three slugs and a dozen mortar fragments in his guts, but he pulled through. And last I heard he was living it up at sixty-two."

"The food's gone," his brother reminded him. "And what about water?"

"Not much left, but we'll manage with tight rationing. A plane could spot us any time; they must be searching. It's only that damned arm of yours that worries me. It has to come off immediately if not sooner. Gotta figure a good way—one you can stand."

"You hard-nosed bastard," Larry said. "Guess you never heard about anesthetics or antibiotics."

"This is only a raft, not the Mayo Clinic. Hell, they even goofed on provisions. It's a wonder the stews got it out of the plane at all. Anyhow, you always claimed to be the toughest of us five."

"I'm a born liar, too."

"Trouble is," Chris said, "no knife. I'll have to try putting an edge on this lid from the food can."

"Great," Larry said, eyeing the metal disc without enthusiasm. "You're full of bright ideas. How about the bone? That's not exactly a chicken wing attached to my shoulder."

Chris blinked. "Damn!" he said. "Forgot all about that, and it's big, too, what with you our family arm-wrestler."

"Lousy suggestion at best," Larry said. He shifted his position, wincing. "Know what? At least we're dying rich."

"What?" Chris demanded. "Oh," he added, remembering. The brothers, five vagabonds, usually broke, but never glum; their first reunion in three years, crowded around the machine at the airport, snatching the insurance forms, taking maximum coverage on lives, arms, legs—the works. Joking and laughing. How could they foresee the broken plane, the flaming tail-section with two brothers in the lounge? The others were supposed to join them for drinks, but never made it; the big jet exploded while they were in the aisle. Some things the survivors could never remember clearly or account for. Why had their part of the stricken plane, instead of plunging straight to the bottom, behaved like a flat stone scaled across a pond, skipping along the water and then floating just long enough for them to scramble out into a tepid sea? And why that one raft emerging from the plane—the work, apparently, of some gallant stewardesses—which then sank immediately, so that the unbearable screams and yells had died out under the water like those in some TV thriller as the audio is artfully lowered? So call it one big miracle, but to what end? They were surely finished.

"Think of all that money," Larry said. "That'll beef up your will to live, even if I can't make it."

Chris knew what his brother meant. Sure, his face was a mess, but unlike gangrene, wouldn't kill him, not if help still came in time—and one brother had to survive.

But Chris wasn't buying that. The arm! The blasted arm! He had to cut it off and give Larry a prayer at least. Nothing to work with; not so much as a rusty razor blade. He scrutinized the horizon despairingly. If only there was a ship in sight ... but how could that be? This was not exactly a busy sea-lane even when surface vessels still sailed these waters. His gaze dropped; he saw the pale fin come closer. How terrible a patience the big brute must have; surely there had to be more promising food around than two men on a raft, out of reach. Then he stiffened, a blazing vision overwhelming him, clear and bright in his imagination. God, what a crazy expedient, but it could work—it had too.

"Larry," he said. "There's a way—if you have the guts." It was a snide approach, but he wanted the kid angry.

His brother peered at him, eyes feverishly bright. He's awful sick, Chris thought. Not much time.

"A way for what?" he asked, moaning as he moved his vastly swollen arm.

"To amputate," Chris said. He pointed seaward, cringing inwardly at what he had to explain. "The shark, Larry. The shark."

His brother's head jerked back; his whole body went rigid.

"Jeez!" he exclaimed. "The sun's finally got you. What the hell about the shark?"

"Remember that Bradley kid in Melbourne? He didn't know his leg was gone until they hauled him aboard and the blood spouted. Didn't feel a thing. It's a terrible thing to ask, but it's the only way I know. It can work. I'll have a tourniquet ready. The arm's killing you. There's nothing to lose, and I want you to live."

There was a brief, highly charged silence. Larry's eyes were slate-colored and not as hard as his brother's, but they held steady.

"I guess you really mean it," he said wonderingly. "Would you do it to yourself? Never mind," he added, before Chris could reply. "I know you would." He turned his head back towards the water where Jack the Ripper still circled the raft. If a shark ever stops moving, it dies, or so he'd heard. No water through its gill slits meant no oxygen for its blood. So endlessly, day and night, the animal must swim on, never knowing prolonged rest.

"I don't seem to have any choice," Larry said, a hum in his voice. "Let's give it a try. As you say, I'm finished unless this arm comes off, so what's to lose?" He examined the gangrened flesh in disgust; God, it stank! "I hope Jack's not a fussy eater."

"Good boy," Chris said, twenty-eight tough years looking down to Larry's somewhat easier nineteen. He'd always kept an eye on the kid brother, but was this trip necessary? Yes—no alternative.

"I'll use my belt for the tourniquet," he said. "You ready, Larry?"

"How do you get ready for a hungry shark?" the boy asked. His face was drained of blood and set like stone. "Let's get it over with."

Chris came over to him, glancing at the shark about ten yards off. The timing would be critical. The big grey had enormous jaws, and unless Larry was pulled back at exactly the right moment a lot more than the bad arm could go. Gently he gripped his brother's good shoulder, then eased the poisoned arm over the stiff rubber gunwale, dipping half of it into the warm water. Larry moaned softly as the salt stung his inflamed flesh. The great predator, sensing the taint of blood, whirled, maneuvered cautiously for perhaps ten seconds, then drove in, fast and deadly.

"Watch it, kid," Chris warned. "None of that baloney about rolling over."

The shark's mouth opened wide, displaying rows of triangular teeth, shiny and hard as surgical steel, just as sharp, and powered by muscles strong enough to make them capable of biting a heavy oar in two. The gaping head shot up from the water, enveloped Larry's arm, and the glittering fangs snapped down with immense force. Instantly Chris whipped his brother back.

"Damn you!" the boy cried, his voice shrill. "I felt that!"

"I know," Chris said softly, busy with his belt on the spouting stump. "You weren't swimming for your life and full of adrenaline. But it was quick and a clean job. I had to, Larry—" But his brother was out cold.

Forty hours later the plane spotted them, and soon after that a navy helicopter carried both to a carrier, where the surgeons peered curiously at the stump.

"How'd that happen?" one asked, and when Chris told him, whistled softly.

Back in the grill, Chris raised his glass. "To Mark, Wally, and Tim," he said. "May their souls be at peace."

"Right," Larry said. A wry smile twisted his lips. "And to Jack the Ripper—Doctor Jack—a mean, cold-blooded son of a bitch—unlicensed, too—but one hell of a surgeon!"

Their glasses clinked together.

Reconstruction

Professor Puffendorf strode into his wife's immaculate bedroom, and something he glimpsed on the polished floor made him stop short in surprise. There, starkly clear on the waxed surface, was a double line of oval marks that spoke volumes to his trained eye—the unmistakable prints of naked feet, big ones.

"*Himmel!*" he exclaimed. "A man—with my Melita!"

The professor had just come back from a fruitful three-day excursion into the Santa Ana foothills, where some remarkable new fossils had been found. He had expected that, as always, Melita would be waiting eagerly for his return, presiding over a huge pan of her superlative egg pancakes. Instead there had been a curt note to the effect that she was spending the weekend with her aunt in Laguna Beach. Leaving the message on the refrigerator had been a further small turn of the screw, a sly reflection on his habits. And, in fact, he had stopped to check the beer even before calling his wife's name.

Aunt in Laguna Beach, indeed! Puffendorf snorted. After seeing the footprints, he was filled with anguished doubt. Never before had Melita failed to await his return at home, as became a dutiful wife. But the past cannot guarantee the future, and the evidence was beyond question. Muttering angrily, he returned his expert gaze to the footprints, and automatically his mind went to work along familiar lines. They were certainly excellent tracks, diamond sharp in the heavy wax. Not even the marks of Melita's slippers could obscure the damning record.

Still acting without conscious reflection, Puffendorf drew a powerful magnifier from his pocket and knelt for a closer scrutiny. What lovely prints; even the pores were visible in the waxy matrix. A wave of anger made his blood race. It was a young man, not more than twenty-three—and she was thirty-eight. Why, such an affair was indecent. Judging from the spread and clarity of detail, the fellow must have weighed about one-seventy-four, plus or minus two—but what was this? The professor drew himself up, full of self-reproach. Hypothesizing with insufficient data. That would never do; it merely showed how shaken he was by Melita's unfaithfulness. One should use a micrometer, make tests with weights on other nearby areas of the wax—his eyes widened suddenly at the import of these thoughts. Yes, by Heaven! He, Puffendorf, the man whose brilliant reconstruction of a new species of Diplodocus had been verified to the last tail-bone by the discovery of a complete, well preserved skeleton, would now apply his unique genius to this homewrecker. He would confront Melita and her young lover with a veritable statue of the seducer, reproducing him almost *en flagrante delicto*, barefoot and approaching—ah, the very idea was agonizing. But justice be done; after that the way was clear for repentance and forgiveness. He had until Monday; for Puffendorf that was ample time. The man who could recreate a giant prehistoric reptile from muzzle to tail-tip in two weeks could certainly do a mere man in three days. He drew a deep, exultant breath and set to work.

It must be confessed that once involved in the ever-fascinating problem of a detailed reconstruction, the professor often lost sight of the depressing end in his enjoyment of the means. There were times when he whistled Strauss cheerfully between his teeth, forgetting momentarily that he was building a replica of Melita's paramour, a villainous young upstart who had cuckolded the great Puffendorf.

His precise measurements of the best prints, his ingenious calibration of the viscosity of the wax by little weights which determined its tendency to spread under pressure, his abstruse mathematics, which corrected the previous data for temperature difference (it was now about ten degrees cooler than when the tracks were made)—all these routines of his profession went smoothly. In a matter of hours he had molded, in his own variety of plastic, using a scale of one to five, the feet, slender, long and shapely; and the legs, superb pillars of bone and muscle, of the culprit. Contrasting these powerful members with his own fat-thickened thighs, the professor felt a sharp twinge of envy, although once he too—but that was years ago.

The torso, its proportions mathematically a complex function of the parts already completed, would take another day; and the head and features, most tricky of all, the supreme tests of virtuosity, perhaps eighteen hours of exacting toil. But the professor retired satisfied. In two more working days he would be looking into the counterfeit presentment of his betrayer. For some moments, lying in bed, unable to sleep, he considered the data in hand. Which of his graduate students—the insolence of some young cub!—weighed one hundred seventy four pounds and had the torso of a Greek god? There was DuChesne—after all he was a French exchange student and came from a country that sneered at morality. No, his legs while sturdy, were slightly bowed. What about the American, Joel Hoffman? A track star, excellent build—no, his feet were quite small for his weight.

Tossing feverishly, the professor thought about Melita. In a series of bittersweet mental images he recalled their first meeting at college. And later how she had taken Anthropology I just to be with him, when she might have had the same three units for Dishwashing II; Detergents and Allied Topics (Prerequisite, DW I.) Dozing finally, he saw her at nineteen with candid blue-grey eyes, so dark they were almost purple, incredibly tiny teeth, and a figure so exciting with its sex-aura that once an elderly, blind scholar, emerging wearily from the stacks, had stopped dead, sniffed the air, and as Melita passed, made tentative, hopeful jabs with his cane. When you considered how attractive she still was, he should have expected to beat off potential seducers with a club. Yet this was the first swine who … Professor Puffendorf, exhausted emotionally and physically, began to snore. In his dreams Melita's lover turned out to be a Piltdown Man, and the paleontologist very offensively told the hairy, cringing fellow that he had just been proved a complete fake and had no right to seduce anybody's wife.

Early the next morning, after numerous calculations and measurements, the professor went to work completing the torso. It was obvious, in view of the stride, that the youth was tall; and certain elements of the prints implied a well-proportioned body. It all fitted together nicely. Puffendorf, however, scowled. No one he knew had a body quite that good. This fellow promised to be the sort of male appearing in the "after" panels of those muscle-building ads. And it was true, he reflected, that college men nowadays were nothing like the old lot back at Gottingen when he and Hans Diekmann used to down forty steins and then raise huge casks so that each might gulp from the bunghole.

The professor rechecked his mathematics, then put the slide rule aside. He grunted sourly. The man, whoever he was, had just the build suggested by his prints. Everything was in order; no other proportions would account for those traces in the wax. The ignorant might scoff, but nobody knew better than Puffendorf that every vertebrate is a unique materialization of some footprints in sandstone—or floor polish. As inexorably as the hand of a clock approaches a given hour, so he was closing in on the likeness of the betrayer.

By the third morning, the youth was complete except for his head; the body undoubtedly was correct—and imposing. Melita hadn't met *him* in faculty circles; that was clear. A chap that handsome and muscular couldn't have much brains, which was a pity. And so young—he felt that most. That Melita might allow another great (and venerable) scientist to make love to her was understandable if not quite excusable. But that she should submit to some boy—very likely a loutish lump who yelled from the bleachers or gobbled popcorn while watching wrestling on TV … It was intolerable!

"*Fiat justicia, ruat coelum,*" he said aloud in melancholy tones, dredging the tag up from long forgotten classical studies in the gymnasium of Imperial Germany.

Then he returned his gaze to the model, waiting like some dumb oracle for its head, identity and tongue.

From the prints had evolved the feet, a neat inversion of nature, that, and a unique relation with no margin for error. From the feet, the ankles; little fallacy possible there either, when controlled by a background like his. And the ankles inevitably are determined by the leg-bones and their inserted muscles. The thighs, shaped in subtle geometrical planes, must relate to the legs just so, one function for the male, another, very similar mathematically, but just different enough (*vive la difference!*) physically to distinguish the sexes in all but borderline cases.

Human anatomy to Puffendorf, armed with the vertebrate dynamics of Raymond, was indeed an exact science. Just as the limit of a continuous function is the same no matter how approached, so the head, the limit similarly of the trunk and members, preexists in their relations. The torso has to merge with the hips and thighs; the rhythmic stride, caught in wax, showed by its pendulum swing a periodicity characteristic of the whole organism. And so it went. In two hours or less, he would stare directly into the carven reproduction of his enemy's face.

Humming an air from Bach's "Suite in B Minor," the professor once more forgot his martyrdom in the pleasures of creative effort. Slowly but precisely, with no false steps, the imposing head grew under his stubby yet moth-delicate fingers. The firm, stubborn chin, the full sensual lips, the straight, heavy nose—soon he would know all.

But the completed features, pink and imposing in plastic, told him nothing. Despite a haunting resemblance to somebody familiar—who? *Who?* No, he had never seen that face before. Melita was in love with a stranger.

He studied the expression and boiled with fury. To an anthropologist the model's emotions were all too clear. The face was like that of a starving man within reach of a luscious repast. The parted lips, tense nostrils, and fixed stare all suggested unmistakably a state of sexual excitement. And the aggressive nose pointed squarely at Melita's bed!

Spitting out a stream of guttural oaths, Puffendorf stepped back for a broader view. The moment he did so, doubt assailed him. Something was wrong, lacking, or out of harmony. *What could it be?* Experience told him that a single detail somewhere was incorrect, but he couldn't locate it specifically. Frowning, he snatched up his sheaf of calculations and began a systematic check.

Ah! What was this? Served him right for hurrying. The fifth dynamic function had a discontinuity, a cusp, on a critical curve. But singularity there was most remarkable—what the devil could it mean, unless ... The professor stiffened, the blood rushing from his face. The mathematics was not altogether new to him, after all. He suddenly remembered how Melita and he, in their youthful enthusiasm for anthropology had pestered their friends for prints of hands and feet, for measurements of extremities, and even dimensions that bordered on indecency—as if data about any human organs were anything to blush at. They had even gone to Grauman's Chinese Theater with its famous footprints in concrete. Those traces of Hollywood celebrities had engendered a theory about the glands of movie stars which was still unprinted—and unprintable. No wonder this situation seemed familiar now.

But this solution of the figurine's disproportion brought no joy to Puffendorf. That he should have to make such a change on his wife's lover was insufferable, too much to expect even of a scientist. But after several minutes of painful self-communion, the anthropologist in the professor won over the outraged husband, and he reluctantly added several ounces of plastic to a central region of the model. Even Louisa May Alcott could have guessed by now just what was on the youth's mind when he left those tracks.

At that moment the professor's unhappy reflections were interrupted by a peal of laughter, and he whirled to see Melita holding on to the bedroom door in a paroxysm of mirth.

"Heinrich!" she gurgled. "That's absolutely marvelous—an exact likeness!" His bewildered expression set her off again. Gasping, she pointed to the model. "And still you don't know him!"

Puffendorf gaped at her. Was such behavior consistent with the circumstances? Was Melita utterly lost to shame?

"Who is he?" the professor gritted, clenching his powerful fingers. "I'll break his damned neck with my own hands!"

"You shouldn't go away so much," she replied with demure irrelevance. "I get lonesome. Once I had a lover. We used to collect footprints together. See what a *man* he was!"

Something began to register in her husband's brain. Was it possible that——? He stepped up to the model, and then turned to the mirror of her vanity table. He gulped. Melita was shrieking with laughter again.

"Yes, my darling—the footprints of a man on his wedding night. I 'collected' them the next morning, long ago. Your prints!" A teasing smile touched her lovely mouth. "Are you still big enough to fill them, I wonder?"

The wrinkles on his forehead suddenly smoothed out. She was wearing an off-shoulder dress he hadn't seen before; her shoulders were smooth and slightly tanned, drawn a little back in a challenging way. Her tiny teeth gleamed behind parted lips, and her breathing became audible.

Professor Puffendorf reached for her, hesitated, then dropped a cloth over the model.

"He had his day; this is mine," he told Melita, taking her in his arms.

Masterpiece

The little man obviously was not sober, but neither was he drunk, although a single additional sip might have made him so. His eyes, soft and warm as melted caramel, shone with sincerity; and his fist, white, chubby, with immaculate nails, thumped the stained bar to emphasize his grievance.

"You don't believe me," he complained to the blonde girl beside him. "*He* doesn't either," with a limp gesture towards the bartender, whose small reptilian eyes seemed to stare past both of them, so blank was his gaze.

The girl smiled, a mere twitch of over-red lips.

"I do, dearie," she said, patting his hand. "Every word. I know when a guy's leveling with me." She squeezed his fingers. Her own were like warm, greasy little sausages, and the man gently inspected one of them in a sort of fuddled wonder. "Buy me another drink, honey."

"You think," he went on doggedly, motioning the bartender to take her order, "that a guy who makes eighty thousand a year wouldn't be found dead in a dive like this. That's the idea, isn't it? That's why you don't believe me."

"But I do believe you, darling. Hope to die." She yawned, making a half-hearted effort to cover her mouth, and then smiled apologetically at his resentful glance.

"Here, damn it!" He fumbled in his wallet. "I know how to convince you or anybody else of anything. Here's a hundred-dollar bill. Take it. Go on—small change to me. Keep it."

The girl's flabby face went white; then a deep flush suffused it, and one hand, red-taloned, reached almost timidly towards the money. The bartender's shallow eyes were aglow; she caught his nearly imperceptible nod. The note vanished into her scuffed, outsize purse.

"Now you'll listen," the little man said with grim complacence. "Money talks. And I'll say it again from the beginning. You're sitting next to the guy who sparks the biggest damn advertising agency in the world: Berrier, Keelyn, McCrae, and King. And I'm the one who handles their top account—'Perfect Cigarettes'. You're smoking 'em, I see. Everybody's smoking 'em. Thanks to me, Jay Humphrey Richards, the best huckster who ever lived."

For the first time the bartender spoke. In a hoarse monotone he said: "I've heard of you. You pulled that stunt with *The Times*."

Richards brightened. "You're damned right! Took the first four pages of *The New York Times*. In the center of each page, and not very large at that—lots of white space to set it off—just the slogan: 'A Fine Day. Light up—and make it Perfect!' Cost a fortune, but it was worth every cent. They didn't like the idea—the publisher and editors, I mean. A paper doesn't want to sell its front page. But when you put enough money on the line anything goes. I'll prove that again tomorrow night, by God!"

"I remember that now," the blonde said, awe in her voice. "My old lady saved the issue; she said it might be worth dough some day."

"Your old lady's smart," Richards grinned. "It might. Did you see the double page spread in *Holiday* last month? 'Your best vacation's coming soon! Light up—and make it Perfect!' All my ideas. That's why I'm worth eighty thousand."

The girl peered furtively into her purse, lips parted, then, as if remembering something, leaned against the little man's arm. He pushed her away, but gently, almost absently. "Relax," he said. "All I want tonight is liquor and somebody to talk to. I'm always like that when one of my really big ones is ready to break. And baby, this is the capstone, the *chef d'oeuvre*. *Finis coronat opus*. Latin for 'masterpiece', Honey." He peered about the shabby room. "We're all alone, by God. I know; you want to close the joint. Okay, but I'll be back tomorrow. That's the big night. Sure, I belong in 'The Grotto' or 'Smirnoffs', not in a crummy hole like this, but you know what? I get fed up with stuffed shirts and their ever-lovin', time-servin', enameled women! I prefer real honest bums like you. *You'd* never talk about getting together to cross-pollinate! Believe it or not, I'm just a farm boy." He laughed harshly. "Some farm—we'd have needed fifty more acres to support a grasshopper." He moved towards the door, swaying just a little. "Tomorrow at eleven forty-six p.m.—that's the Zero Hour, kids. Don't miss it." He left.

As soon as the little man was gone, the bartender leaned toward the blonde. He held out one damp, broken-knuckled hand, palm up. For a moment she stared at him defiantly, and even threw one longing glance at the door. Then tears filled her eyes, smearing her face with mascara, and she opened the purse. She put the hundred-dollar bill in his hand, and with a single thin wail, like a beaten puppy, ran out, teetering grotesquely on over-high heels. His face expressionless, the bartender studied the bill under a naked light bulb for several seconds, turning it over twice. Then with a curt nod, he slipped it into his wallet. A moment later he began methodically to turn off the few lights.

At eleven-thirty the following night, the little man returned. Apparently he had paused elsewhere, for he walked with elaborate caution, as if on eggs. The blonde, who had been waiting anxiously all day, hurried forward, and he gave her a bleary grin.

"All set, baby? Blow in that hundred already?" She sniffled, flashing a poisonous glare at the bartender.

Richards looked around the room, and a petulant twist distorted his small pink mouth. In one corner a middle-aged laborer sat at a table with two blowsy women. A boy, unmistakably under eighteen, sat at the bar, his bony, sullen face flushed. These were the only customers. The little man sighed. "The bastard's even smoking Camels," he said gloomily. "Hell of a start." He turned to the bartender, whose iron face relaxed momentarily into a welcoming grimace. "I won't have much of a bunch to celebrate with," Richards complained. "Maybe we ought to round up a few strays. Here." He took out his wallet, and as the girl and the bartender fixed unwinking eyes on it, pulled out a handful of bills. "Drinks on the well-known agency of Berrier, Keelyn, McCrae, and King. But get somebody in here to liven up this morgue, for Chrisakes!"

"Sorry, Mac," the proprietor said. "A slow night. Haven't taken in enough to pay my light bill. You won't find any strays around now. Maybe when the movie lets out."

"Movie!"

"The Empire. A block down."

"When does the show end?"

The bartender shrugged, but the blonde said eagerly: "Near midnight, honey."

"Too damned late," the little man objected. "They'll miss the fun. At least, they'll miss the premiere—the psychological moment. The hills block the view here in the valley; I should have gone ..." His voice dwindled to a fretful murmur.

"What fun?" the bartender demanded, without much interest. He had already taken the crumpled bills from the bar, and a flicker of surprise crossed his face. Big stuff—fifties and hundreds. He studied the advertising man more carefully in the poor light, noticing for the first time his expensive suit with its bloom like that of a moth. The little guy must be the McCoy after all. He took quite a chance, running around in places like this with his pockets full of century notes. A skinny shrimp, too.

"What fun?" Richards repeated blearily. "I told you, damn it. Tonight's my crowning achievement. And that's saying a lot. I'm the boy who imported thirty thousand dollars worth of Mexican coins and stamped 'em 'The Perfect way to spend money'. Got around the silly American currency laws very neatly. Can't deface money, Washington says. I didn't see anybody unhappy about getting this batch, defaced or not. But the Nice Nellies in the Treasury Department took 'em all up on some technicality; bullied the Mexican officials, too. Well, we had our money's worth in publicity. That year we topped American Tobacco.

"You see? I'm a genius. That's why I get sick of stuffed shirts who just re-word other peoples' ideas. I'd sooner talk to the man in the street—and the street walker, dear—they're genuine.

"Did I tell you? I'm the one who painted 'A Fine View—Make it Perfect!' on the White Cliffs of Dover. Visible miles out to sea. We went round and round with His Majesty's Government on that one. All through their medieval courts. Their judges wear wigs like oil mops, so help me. They made us scrub it off, and I never got a chance to try my 'England Expects Every Smoker' gimmick. Had a helluva good suggestion about Mount Rushmore, too, but—what time is it?"

The bartender looked at his wrist. "Quarter to twelve. No watch, Mac? How come, a big shot like you? I can get you a beauty. Swiss make, but no tax."

"No watch!" Richards was indignant. "I'll show you." He downed his martini in one gulp, and reached into a pocket. The blonde gave a little gasp of pure covetousness, and the bartender leaned forward. It lay on the greasy wood, a flat, exquisite thing, glittering with gems and rich with colored enamel inlays. A dozen tiny dials covered the face, which was intricately engraved.

"By L. Leroy and Company of Paris," Richards said proudly. "Made in 1901 and cost me 250,000 francs in 1948."

"Lookit all the little hands," the blonde said, naive wonder in her voice.

"This is really a watch, honey. Days of the week; date of the month; seasons; phases of the moon; apparent solar time; full striking, minutes repeater on three gongs—listen." He pressed a tiny stud, and faint chimes sounded, sweet and melodic, like church bells at an infinite distance. "Boreal and astral skies; sunrise; sunset—you name it."

"I'll be damned," the bartender said, and the youth, leaving his stool, edged closer, bony jaws working. Naked avarice showed in his pale eyes. The bartender drove him back with a cold, menacing stare.

"By God!" Richards cried suddenly. "We're blabbing here as if time didn't matter. Outside—quick! Or we'll miss the premiere. You'll want to tell your kids about seeing *this* opening, believe me."

The full force of his driving, relentless ego abruptly mastered them, and even the bartender shuffled after him to the sidewalk. The movie crowd was just streaming by. The night air was balmy with summer; they could smell the pungent, subtly disturbing odor of jasmine. Without knowing it, the bartender and the blonde girl drew closer together, as if anticipating something momentous.

The little man held up the watch, twisting it irritably. "One thing they didn't have then," he grumbled. "Luminous dials." He fumbled for a match and struck it on his shoe. "Any second now," he said, peering down. "This'll set the boys back on their heels. Only Berrier, Keelyn, McCrae, and King could have swung a deal like this. Thanks to me, Jay Richards—and money enough to buy back Manhattan Island. They'll forget Barnum ever lived after tonight," he added, squaring his narrow shoulders. "There she comes."

He pointed to where the pine-topped hills bulked dark against the starry midsummer sky. A silver mist sprayed the furry ridges with magic light. The theatre crowd seemed to pause in its gay progress down the street as the sharpest eyes became fixed. Somebody called out in shrill, excited tones; there were little cries and nervous giggles. A man said loudly: "Mother, put on your glasses, quick!"

Another voice, deeper, and touched with a kind of surprised petulance, rose above the general murmur: "Damned if I can figure it after thirty years of engineering. Must be an optical illusion, by George, though just how—" And the higher teenage retort, full of young assurance: "It's the new Polaris Rocket, Dad, a three stager—some sweet job. Got an electronic brain that'll land it on a dime even out there. A pattern of 'em set to spill trails of dark powder would do it, all right. Jeez—over craters an' everything, just like neat printing. And no wind or rain to spoil it, ever."

"Queen of the Night," the advertising man shouted, pointing. "*Finis coronat opus*," he repeated thickly.

The great black letters sprawled over harsh, sun-drenched dead seas and gaunt, precipitous mountain chains …

A LOVELY EVENING
LIGHT UP—AND MAKE IT PERFECT!

Morning After

When he awoke, it was still dark, and his first thought was: "What a brawl—man!" Certainly the affair last night had been almost too typical to be true. Even Melita Marlowe's shoulder straps had slipped on schedule, proving what everybody knew, that she never wore a bra except when performing for the blind.

Larry rolled over and peered at Gwen in the dim glow of the night-light. All he could see was her tousled auburn hair; the rest of her slender body was deep curled under the fuzzy blue blankets. And no wonder, he thought, with a shiver; it was damned chilly this morning; unusually so, even for the ranch with its desert climate.

He rolled back towards the night table, trying to make his sleep blurred eyes, with their greatly enlarged pupils, focus on the illuminated dial of the clock. Six thirty. Must be only six thirty in the morning. He cocked his head quizzically. That didn't make much sense. The party hadn't broken up until four. Eight to four—a real gasser. After that, Gwen and he had stopped for hotcakes, and didn't get to bed until five. And even then, excited by the sights and sounds of the uninhibited bash, with its gorgeous girls and sleek boys right from the biggest studios, they had made love themselves, with an enthusiasm and rapport never before achieved in their brief marriage.

But surely, Larry reflected, pulling the blanket about his throat, he must have slept more than a lousy hour or so. Why, both of them had been doubly pooped by the long night of gaiety and the tension-release of love. He muttered something in his puzzlement, and Gwen stirred, giving a little moan. Then she was awake, staring at him with those huge, greenish eyes that made everybody think of her as a tawny, youthful cat. Looking at her, as she lay there quietly, a cryptic smile on her mouth, he thought again of how lucky they both were. It was wonderful to be so young, healthy, attractive, with a creative profession and a stunning wife like Gwen. The way those movie and TV wolves had surrounded her, you'd think their own dates were witches instead of the most toothsome starlets the big studios had under contract. And Gwen didn't need trick shoulder straps, either. It was that inner light; the sort of thing Garbo had, and Bergman. Best of all, it burned only for her husband. Here was one young beauty who didn't thirst for a screen career. Not even when Mapes and Horowitz and Brandt all offered her one on a silver platter.

Luckily Larry's own career didn't depend on his wife's attractions. As the top young TV writer in the West, he always had more commissions than he could execute, even though he could turn out a slick half hour teleplay in one afternoon.

Yes, Larry thought, smiling back at Gwen, it's a case of ceiling unlimited. Haberman was sure Larry's play would be produced on Broadway. If it was a hit—and the chances were excellent—future possibilities were staggering. No morning could be grey enough to lower his spirits. Not while he had his talent and Gwen.

"What time is it, darling?" she asked him.

"Six thirty, dear. A drizzly, cold day in prospect, it looks like."

"What do you expect in January, even in California? But I'll bet it's better in the Valley—maybe even sunny. Why are we living in this God-forsaken place a hundred miles from nowhere?"

"Because I hate crowded cities," he told her, not for the first time. "And admit it honestly, Gwen—you're beginning to like the ranch yourself."

"That's true," she said, stroking his cheek lightly with one finger. "The hills and the wildflowers really send me. But it is awfully isolated."

"Nothing's that bad with a telephone. Besides, a writer thrives on isolation."

For a moment he peered towards the window, and his thick eyebrows arched momentarily.

"It's mighty damned dark out there. You know, Gwen, it's just occurred to me that we must have slept right through Sunday morning and afternoon. I'll bet anything it's six thirty p.m., not a.m. at all."

"But that's—let me see—over twelve hours. I've never slept that long in my life."

"I know. But we were both worn out. I wouldn't wake up after a lousy hour or so. Neither would you. If it's a case of one hour or twelve, it has to be twelve."

"You must be mistaken," she objected, sitting up and hugging her knees under the blankets. "It wouldn't be this dark in the early evening."

"Remember they predicted heavy rain today."

"I know, but Larry, it's a night-time dark, not a cloudy one. Just look at the hills."

He slipped out of bed, wincing at the cold air, and went to the window. "That's odd. I can see quite a few stars. You must be right, after all. It certainly can't be so dark at six thirty just because of clouds, and still have a starry sky. But, dammit, Gwen, I just don't feel like a man who's had only a short nap. I'm wide awake, and rested clear through."

"So am I, darling," she admitted. "But it's just nervous tension. You know how it is when a person's too tired to sleep sometimes. A sort of bright, dry alertness. You feel full of energy, and not a bit sleepy, but nevertheless your body can be completely exhausted. It hits you later, like an avalanche. Still, I must say it doesn't feel like that. Why don't we find out for sure if it's a.m. or p.m.?"

"How?"

"I don't know. We could call Tom and Ann."

"Like hell. And let them think we're so befuddled or full of liquor we can't tell morning from evening? You know dear old Tom, the practical joker; we'd never hear the last of it."

"What about the newspapers? They're up all night, and always answering questions."

"That'd be worse. They'd smell a story—human interest stuff—and we'd be on Page One. 'Big TV Writer Doesn't Know What Time It Is. Hollywood Party Leaves Larry Trent in Fourth Dimension'."

"It's so cold," Gwen complained. "That before-the-dawn chill. Why is it always so chilly these days?"

"Who knows? Weather runs in cycles. They say we're in for a long spell of below average temperatures. Sunspots or something."

"We're both silly," she said. "What's wrong with Time Service? After all, that's what it's for."

"Never heard of it."

"Why should you, with a dozen clocks in the house? It's Time Service, you darling dunce. By the telephone company. Just dial Cathedral 1-4000, and get the exact time, day or night. It'll cost only one dime added to our bill."

"Don't use that awful word, 'bill'. Our heat is costing us fifty per cent more this year."

"But you're getting a hundred per cent more for everything you write," she reminded him. "We mustn't complain. We're too damned lucky as it is. A few years ago it looked like war with Russia; now things are quiet." She shivered. "Only a new ice age to worry about. Good thing we both ski. Now go ahead and try Time Service, like a good boy."

"I didn't know they had such a thing," Larry said, "but that's the answer, all right."

He pulled the phone nearer the night-light, and dialled. There was a click, several whirs, and a cool voice announced: "At the sound of the musical note, it will be exactly six forty-three."

"Hey," Larry cried. "Six forty-three what? Is it a.m. or p.m.? Operator—"

"You're wasting your time," Gwen said, with a giggle. "It's just a recording, silly. You don't think some poor girl's going to sit there all night telling people the time."

"But it's no damned good," Larry objected. "She didn't say a.m. or p.m. We know the hour without her help."

"Well," his wife said sweetly, "you mustn't blame them for assuming the subscriber knows that much, at least. I mean, whether it's morning or evening. Come back to bed before you freeze. After all, it has to be one or the other. If we doze for a while, it will get lighter or darker—simple, yes?"

"Not with the crazy grey days lately. Too much fog or clouds. I'm sure it's a.m., but now I've just got to know, or I'll go nuts. I certainly couldn't sleep any more. I feel as if I've been dead to the world for at least six hours—maybe ten—but then all the clocks can't be wrong. Blast it all! I have to settle this. Hey, what about TV? Where's the guide?"

"You forget the set went dead on Wednesday. I asked you to get the repairman right away, but you said Tom would fix it on Friday. When you hire somebody, the job gets done. Ask a friend to do it for free—"

"All right, already," Larry said. "You win. Do we have a radio in the house?"

"Not since you jumped on it. I think you said that when the no-talent singers got so bad that even the commercials were a relief—"

"You and your total recall! Well, what's the answer then?"

"Better try the operator—the live one."

"She'll think I'm crazy."

"Undoubtedly, my pet. But she won't say so. They're trained to be impossibly tactful and noncommittal. I had a cookie friend once who tried for weeks to heckle an operator into breaking up—wild gags, the most hilarious accents; the works. All he got was a lecture from some supervisor with a voice that would frost up a steam table. Finally they took his phone out. For all I know, he's using signal flags."

"Okay," Larry said, with a grimace. "The operator it is." He dialled 113, and before anybody could respond, hastily offered his defense. "Listen, Operator, I'm not trying to be cute, and please don't think I'm crazy, but my wife and I got to bed very late last night—this morning—and just woke up. I know it sounds silly, but with the goofy weather lately, and all the dark days, we can't tell a thing from looking outside. Just clear up one point. Is it—let me see—six forty-nine a.m. or p.m.?"

There was a long, unnatural moment of dead silence. Then Larry felt his neck hairs prickle. A thin titter of laughter was coming over the line. He was not indignant; for there was no ridicule in it; the girl was not amused at his plight. Rather, it was hysteria born of terror. He couldn't know that the operator sat there alone, deserted at her post, fulfilling her duties like an automaton; that, unlike her fellow employees, she was too disoriented to seek the comfort of home, church, or the jammed streets. Nor could he, from the isolated ranch, be aware of the chaos of fear and license that was Los Angeles. With his eyes fixed on the smiling face of his wife, who had not yet noticed the change on his own, he heard the girl sobbing at her switchboard.

She was saying: "... so you slept through ... and missed the announcements ... you were lucky ... didn't even know ... that the sun went out at five on Sunday ... they say it won't ever shine again ..."

Night of the Puppet

Police Chief Kent Nolan got the bad news at two in the morning. Victim number eighteen had been found dead, just like the others, with no detectable cause of death. But there was more to it than that: the murdered man was an old friend; in fact, they had worked their way up through the ranks together, and had even married sisters.

The chief was a huge man, two hundred and forty pounds of bone and muscle. It was told of him that as a rookie, frustrated by two hoods holed up in a garage and firing at everything in sight, he had scaled a manhole cover like some giant frisbee against the heavy door, smashing it open and almost pulverizing the men inside. The story was apocryphal, but many people who saw Nolan in action believed it.

And now, hearing the news, he sat alone in his private office, haggard from weeks of long hours and merciless strain, and wept. Only a few tears came, then the grief sank deep into his heart, leaving nothing outside to attract notice. The buck stopped at Nolan's desk; there was no time for mourning; rather there were eighteen people— men, women, even a child—to be avenged. Or if he rejected that notion, as a good cop must, they had to be used as a basis for stopping the terrible sequence of killings. A nightmarish series, no matter how one looked at it. No motives, no ties among the victims, no discernable cause of deaths. The only constant was that of locations; all the murders had occurred in a shabby residential area near the old warehouse district.

Going over the records for the hundredth time, the chief rubbed his reddened eyes and scowled. Nothing made any sense. Surely after the first few killings nobody in his right mind would wander off into an alley or dark street alone at night; there had been plenty of warnings.

Yet, however unbelievable it seemed, the latest victims must have done just that.

Then there were the idiotic and useless coroners' reports. Apparently all those people had died of sheer exhaustion—how absurd! No wounds, no poison, no drugs; the medicos refused to budge on that. All they could find for sure was some kind of massive debility, as if the victims had simply over-exerted themselves. That might make sense, Nolan reflected wearily, if there were also signs of terror— flight from imminent death or—or what? A monster? But that wasn't the case; none of the dead had expressions other than placidity; hell, they might have been killed sleeping! And what about the needle-marks on the wrists? That was a constant, too; he shouldn't forget it, even if no coroner would swear to a significant loss of blood. Some people have more than others, they pointed out; how can we tell? No matter, the chief thought; what person in normal health would collapse over losing a pint of blood or even two? Some of the smaller women, maybe; or the one twelve-year-old boy, but not the others, all husky males. Burly guys from the factory area where they worked. Sighing, he shoved the thick file away, wondering what he could possibly say at the coming conference with his men—a council of desperation at this point.

At the meeting next morning he stuck his neck out a country mile to say firmly, quelling his own doubts, "No use griping about the medical examiners. We've had independent verdicts, and nobody found any poison. 'Signs of extreme exhaustion'—that's all they came up with. Just as if they'd been running like crazy—only none of them moved more than a few feet as far as we can tell. I'm no doctor, but I feel we still can't rule out some kind of tricky drug is involved. Which leads to the real baffler: how does the killer still get people to meet him alone after dark in secluded places? We've issued constant warnings on TV and in all the other media. I just don't get it; there must be some reason we're missing. Any ideas?"

"What about the needle-marks?" a sergeant asked. "On every victim's wrist, sometimes right, sometimes left."

"I don't know," was the frank reply. "As to which wrist, that's obvious. Right-handed people get it on the right; left-handed on the left. Must mean something, but what?"

He looked at them challengingly. They were obviously worn out, as he was. The lunatic murderer had taken the starch out of these veteran cops. Pooped, he thought, but not beaten; a good bunch.

"There's another thing," a lieutenant said. "Why haven't our decoys ever worked? We've sent out men, women, even kids— damned near; over eighteen, of course, but small and young-looking— and not one attempt on them. How does the guy know they're covered?"

"A good question," Nolan said wryly. "Wish I could answer it. Wish I could answer any question about this case," he added.

"So where does that leave us, Captain?"

"Where cops usually are—in the soup. The public's screaming like a scalded eagle, and the press is getting really vicious. Can we blame 'em? Eighteen murders, and not a single lead!"

"Are we really sure there's no motive?" the Commissioner demanded. "Blood may have been drawn. It's a nutty angle, but men have killed for crazier reasons."

"The doctors don't agree on that, either," Nolan said. "You simply can't tell, when a person's dead, whether he's lost a fairly small amount of blood. If they'd been drained dry, that'd be one thing, but— " He shrugged. "Certainly, if blood was taken, it can't be for profit; that's really wild. Some of the victims had enough money in their wallets or purses for a gallon of blood, and yet nothing was stolen."

"Then what's your next move?" the Commissioner asked. There was a wiry edge in his voice that the chief recognized. Unless they got results soon the department would have a new captain. So be it; he was ready for a last try.

"We'll have to use single decoys," Nolan said. "No covering at all; on their own." The men exchanged wondering glances, and he added quickly, "I know it's risky as hell, but no women, of course; only well-trained young men in top condition. Close combat experts; all we can find." He thought there was a relaxation among the older, more portly officers, and gave the group a wintry smile. "They'll have to be ready for just about anything; the operation's a shot in the dark, as we all realize, but maybe this time we'll finally flush the killer out."

Having expected this contingency, and quietly prepared for it, Chief Nolan was able to round up a cadre of men fast. They were all tough, young, vigorous cops, most of them veterans of recent wars, and familiar with every kind of dirty fighting. He sent them out feeling for the first time that a break was due. Surely the mad killer couldn't sucker any of these tough kids.

But the outcome was pure disaster, far worse than anybody had thought possible. Some thought the murderer might show and then run, getting away clean, with only one man to elude. Others guessed he'd be too wary to close with a cop. What nobody foresaw was that three husky officers, good at karate, well armed with .38 specials, home from a war that taught or killed, would wind up as dead as the feeblest of the civilian victims. Twenty-one murders, and still no leads.

Nolan's scowl, it was said, would paralyze a felon at fifty yards, and now, as he locked himself up in his office, it was more fearsome than ever. He meant to go over the records again, down to the last punctuation mark. He drew on years of hard-bought experience, the intuition of a born cop, and the wolverine courage of his nature.

It was in the second and fourteenth killings that he spotted one minor factor they had in common; he clutched at it as a drowning man claws at a floating chip before sinking. Both reports mentioned a child—a very young one. A Mrs. Kramer, old and ill, standing at her window in the throes of an asthmatic attack, told the police that shortly before a man's body was found in the alley she had glimpsed a little girl—"a mite, not more than three, officer, in a white dress ... but it was quite dark ..."

Blearily, Nolan thought about it. A baby girl, alone at one a.m., near a deserted alley. Certainly, that wasn't normal. Yet the cruiser, arriving very promptly, didn't find a child around.

Nolan turned to the other case. Again a small girl, also in white— "it looked like a nightdress," the witness had said. "I went out to shoo away some noisy cats, and saw her. Funny thing, too; she was carrying a big, red balloon; that puzzled me. You don't think of kids and balloons in the middle of the night. But I saw her plain, under the street-lamp. Then, all of a sudden, she was gone."

The captain stirred, becoming more alert in spite of bone-deep fatigue. Could the lure be a child? The notion was strangely repellant. A three-year-old trained to decoy men—and women—to their deaths? And if so, why? In God's name—why? Not for a few ounces of blood.

There was the problem of location, too. Those places where the girl—or some girl—had been seen were miles apart, so obviously she didn't actually live at both. That meant she was being transported. For that matter, there was little pattern to the killings. Near the warehouse area, to be sure, but along a border of six miles.

All right, Nolan told himself. Suppose the kid *is* a lure. An ordinary citizen, even warned, might follow her into a dark alley, stupid as such behavior clearly was. People had no sense when it came to cute children. But the policemen, briefed and alert? They might go along, but only with extreme caution, guns ready, expecting the adult killer behind it all, and watching every shadow. None of them should have died, and surely not without a struggle. What kind of murderer could kill a trained cop who was keyed up for trouble? And yet that, if the medics were right, is exactly what had happened; knocked off like so many sheep.

A police chief has no business fighting in the ranks, but Nolan was sick of desk work, of sending others out to die; besides, his job was on the line, so what could he lose? He'd go it alone, hoping for a break. He'd been lucky before, like the time, just on a hunch, he'd looked for Joe Kelly at the ice-show …

There was one thing he kept to himself. Doctor Bond had given him some new kind of benzedrine, great for licking fatigue. If there really was a question of exhaustion as a factor in the murders, this was a way to tilt the odds. Not that any child could wear him down in a chase; it was unthinkable; in spite of the long grind, he was strong and vigorous.

For ten days his lonely walks led to nothing, but on the eleventh Nolan got his break. He was covering a last block to the north, paralleling the warehouse district, when he saw the tiny, white figure appear just ahead. It was as if she had fallen from the skies, so abruptly did she enter his field of vision. As he blinked in surprise, she came closer in an odd, gliding motion. His neck-hairs prickled momentarily until he saw that she was, after all, only a little girl, bare-footed and wearing a white nightgown. She can't be over three, he told himself in dismay, and almost naked in the chilly damp.

But he wasn't going to be trapped, no matter how pathetic the lure. Behind her was the killer, he knew, and Nolan watched in every direction including straight up. Nobody would take him without a real fight!

She came closer, sobbing, but her face, he noted, was remarkably undistorted. She's acting, all right, he told himself; some bastard's really taught her. In a light, clear voice she sang: "I'm lost! Please help me, Mister. I wanna go home!"

"So that's the pitch!" he thought exultantly, still scanning the whole scene, every nerve tingling. But nobody else was near; he could see clearly, so bright was the moon. She would have to lead him to the murderer, just as with the other poor devils. One, Benson, had been a sex pervert, a child-molester, and how happy the clown must have been to have a victim actually seek him out; what irony. But Benson wouldn't follow a kid home; he'd want her to go with him … Besides, the bodies lay just about where they had fallen, so—? Damn it; no sense to the business even yet.

The girl held out a beseeching hand, so tiny, pink, and chubby. It was a confiding gesture, and Nolan extended his own fingers. Too late he realized the fatal blunder. Her grip was like the closing of a compound pliers-wrench, biting into his palm with immense force. Fool! He berated himself. You damned fool! But no matter; let her cling; he could tear her away with his other hand.

But when he tried, there was no strength left. Some terrible mechanism in the tiny hand vibrated and glowed, sucking the vitality from him so fast that he slumped to the sidewalk, unable to move. The child's grasp relaxed; she shifted her hold to his wrist, a large needle rising from her palm. It drove deep into the big vein, and he saw muzzily, with more wonder than fear, how a membranous sack swelled up as it filled with his blood. She must have taken several pints before the needle flipped back into its recess. She drifted away a few yards, then, to his amazement, there was a faint humming and the child soared into the air, lightly as any bubble. No wonder, he thought, we never found her near the bodies … straight up, upsy daisy she goes … where, nobody knows …

He should have been dead, of course, like all the others, and not a witness, but his huge, healthy body and the three benzedrine tablets he'd taken a few hours earlier made a critical difference this time. He watched the little figure sail up to the roof of a long-abandoned warehouse and knew that the killer had to be there.

It was only two blocks away, but every inch became a struggle right from a nightmare, the kind where clinging, invisible muck makes free movement nearly impossible. But he got there, finally, went through a gaping hole in one wall, and up the corroded iron stairs to the roof.

He took the .38 special out of its holster, and staggered across the peeling tar-paper to where something glistened green under the moon. It was some kind of starship, he realized, and badly crumpled. And outside—God in heaven! A thing that fizzed and rippled as he approached. Never of this world, Nolan told himself, oddly calm now. From Somewhere Else; trapped, sending out that horrible little puppet to fetch blood. A perfect lure, a girl-child lost and afraid. No wonder people got suckered.

The fizzing rose in pitch, and the girl came running towards him, interposing her small body between Nolan and her master—her builder, operator—who had undoubtedly contrived the little android from material in the wrecked ship. No telling her own powers, the chief knew; he dare not risk closing with her.

His will made a last, unreasonable demand on his magnificent body, and it responded. Nolan swung his right leg in a mighty kick; the heavy shoe caught the simulacrum squarely below the breastbone. It was not human flesh under his toes; the impact told him that, and more. The puppet hurtled through the air, over the parapet, and dropped five stories to the concrete below. No flying mechanism sustained it this time; something had been disrupted by the powerful kick. The figurine of a child in white fell like a stone and was shattered. Only the head remained intact; later a warehouse worker found it, and his wife made a rag body to fit, much to the delight of their daughter.

Still holding death at arm's length for a few necessary seconds, Nolan leveled the revolver and took careful aim. He caught one glimpse of something like a stalked eye, faceted and glowing in the dark. Then he squeezed the trigger until the gun was empty.

The fizzing dropped in pitch, wavered, then stopped. Nolan sank to his knees, completely numb and cold. But before he died he saw the eye lose its luminescence, and knew that the alien was finished, too.

Three months later at a testimonial dinner the Police Commissioner said: "There's only one answer. Chief Nolan must have tracked the killer to some hideout, probably in the warehouse district. They exchanged fire and both men died. I still think we're bound to find the bodies eventually; it's just that the place is lousy with abandoned buildings, all big, and a thorough search takes time. But the killings have stopped, so I think that's how it was."

But within two weeks there occurred the long expected Quake of the Century, a terrifying 8.6 on the Richter Scale, and many old buildings collapsed. Both Nolan's body and the starship were buried under tons of rubble. Years later, an Urban Renewal crew, bulldozing the ruins, briefly debated some fragments of green metal, finally deciding they were corroded copper, covered with verdigris. Farther down, they discovered identifiable human remains, and Kent Nolan received a more proper burial.

And the rag doll, still cherished by her owner, now middle-aged, has a place of honor near the picture window. Her small head is crammed with marvelous devices nobody dreams are there, and she still wears that expression, serene but enigmatic, as if waiting, with endless patience, for some message from the stars.

Man's Best Friend

All the people on Lennox Avenue pitied Joe Caldwell, suspected the morals of his blonde wife, Lotta, and detested their vicious dog, Rex.

Joe was small, pale, and ineffectual.

Lotta was big, noisy, and overbearing.

Rex, a large, smooth-coated Irish terrier, was bad tempered, enormously egotistical, and a fussy feeder. He adored his indulgent mistress and tyrannized over her. His real slave, however, was the man of the house. Rex enjoyed bullying him.

Every evening, at precisely six thirty, Joe Caldwell went to the corner newsstand for a paper. Although he believed himself to be walking the dog, it was obvious to the world that the big terrier was in charge. He weighed almost as much, and had far more iron in his system. Occasionally Caldwell was permitted to cover the one long block from house to corner in ten minutes; but more often, twenty-five was par for the course, since Rex had a number of favorite detours, mostly sanitary, along the route.

Usually, somewhere along the block, they met Tom Blake, also bound for the newsstand. The two men would have enjoyed chatting, having certain ideas in common about custom-built rifles, although Caldwell seldom fired one, since Lotta hated guns. But their conversations never lasted more than a few minutes. By that time, snarling and tugging at his leash, Rex adjourned the meeting.

Blake never protested, nor did he make a suggestion long cherished and dear to his heart—one having to do with the violent application of a baseball bat to Rex's plump red body. He knew, as did all the neighborhood, that the terrier was better fed and more civilly treated at home than his master; and that if Caldwell ever raised so much as a finger against Lotta's darling—well, nobody could foretell the exact consequences, but the little man himself was certainly not up to them.

So, with a wary eye on Rex's viciously wrinkled lips, and the telltale flattening of his crumpled left ear, Blake would edge away. He could not help feeling that Joe's control of the dog was at best shaky. The animal's immense ego dwarfed his master's. And Blake had no baseball bat handy. It followed that their discussion of duplex loading was never carried very far.

Since it was universally accepted that poor little Joe Caldwell had neither the spirit nor the strength to revolt against his position of low third in a family of two, Blake was astonished and pleased to hear the news.

"Gone?" he repeated feebly. "Joe Caldwell—gone?"

Grinning, the newsboy nodded. "Skipped out yesterday. Him *an'* the dog. That blonde floozie o' his must be wild by now. No more meal ticket. She was bad enough this morning, they say. He'd just better not come back, is my idea."

"She misses the terrier, I suppose," Blake said dryly. "It couldn't be Joe she wants back—for himself, I mean. But why in hell did he take the dog? I always figured Joe hated that damn nasty hound."

"Sure he did. Everybody knows that," the newsboy agreed, with a smirk.

"Ah," said Blake.

"Yeah—you get it." He slid an extended finger across his throat. "Bet old Rex is at the bottom o' the river by now. An' good riddance, too."

"And we thought Joe didn't have it in him." Tom shook his head wonderingly.

"That's what everybody's been yakkin', but I say a guy can only take so much, see? Don't matter how easy-goin' he is. With his wife makin' up to every man in sight, an' a mean ol' dog gettin' better treatment at home than him—hell! He jus' hadda, that's all."

"When you put it like that," Blake agreed, folding his paper, "it does make sense, I'll admit. Me, I'm mighty tickled that Joe skipped. I'd have done it years ago."

Nevertheless, on reaching his home, he made a last wistful survey of the street, half hoping to spot a small man making doubtful erratic progress with a huge, surly dog.

A week later, on his way to the newsstand a few moments behind schedule, Blake met the newcomers. It happened rather suddenly. He was lost in thought, walking mechanically, when there was a violent tug at his pants, and he looked down, startled, to see a tiny white poodle. The animal, emaciated, dirty, and trembling, pawed at him in a frenzy, whimpering with excitement.

He stooped to pat the pathetic creature with its pleading, eloquent eyes, but it was jerked away with a vicious tug. The poodle gave an agonized yelp, and Blake, furious, raised his eyes. A bulky, red-haired man was glaring at him belligerently.

"Ex pug," was Blake's mental comment as he spotted the cauliflower left ear, crumpled and thick with scar tissue. "Aching for a fight, too. Man, what a husky, mean-looking brute!"

"Keep your damn paws off my dog!" the big man snarled, baring strong, white teeth. He had, Blake noticed, unusually large canines. "And you, Joey—!" He whaled the cringing animal with a doubled segment of the leather leash. "I'll learn you to stay at heel and lay off strangers."

Blake guessed it was done deliberately to provoke him, but refused to take the bait. This trained bruiser could flatten him with a single punch, and obviously enjoy doing it. The miserable poodle, still trying to reach Tom, whined and yelped under a rain of punishing blows. Blake set his teeth, longing for a baseball bat. He'd love to give this pug a mate to that bad ear. Then he shrugged, sidestepped, and continued on his way, ignoring a fleering laugh behind him.

Still seething, he questioned the newsboy.

"Who's that big, red-haired hoodlum with the poodle? New around here, isn't he?"

"Him? Yeah. Blew in a few days ago. Thought you knew about him. He comes down the street every night about this time."

"A nasty specimen. Tried to pick a fight with me just now."

"He's a bastard," the newsboy said flatly. "*Mr.* King." He sneered. "An' if you leave off the 'Mr.', he'd just as soon clout you as not. Wasn't for my bad leg, he'd o' pasted me the other night. An' me pushin' sixty! Imagine that big ape takin' over after Joe Caldwell."

Blake gulped.

"Sure. Didn't you hear about it? He's the one. Lotta speaks soft to *him*, they tell me. This time the dog gets it from all sides, poor little mutt. Funny switch, hey?"

"Happened awful fast, didn't it? Why, nobody even knows where Joe is. A man from the collection bureau claims there's no record of his leaving town at all. You'd wonder how a guy like that learned to get away without a trace. But legally, Joe and Lotta are still—"

"Huh!" the newsboy interrupted scornfully. "Nothin' legal about this deal between King an' her. He moved in, that's all. Just like—" he spat—"a couple o' dogs!"

Secret Vice

Felix was eating potato salad and planning the murder of his fifth wife. The previous four, through their insurance policies and savings, had made him wealthy; but expenditure has a habit of growing faster than income, so Felix had again become a family man. Not for long, however.

Some people will tell you that banks and insurance companies are difficult to defraud. But no. In the case of Felix he had disposed of four wives by means of drowning (accidental, of course); electrocution (the old why-did-she-monkey-with-that-heater-while-bathing? trick); a fatal slip on a newly-waxed floor (yes, officer; you see where her poor head hit the edge of that table); and heart failure (a neat use of drugs).

Since all of these tragedies had taken place in widely separated communities, and involved policies from different companies, there had been no breath of suspicion. Besides, Felix always took out a similar policy, in favor of his wife, on himself. That made the whole situation seem very normal.

Then, too, he was canny enough to control his greed, and keep the insurance reasonably small. Ten thousand dollars was a gratifying amount of cash to inherit, and any old hag of a wife was worth at least that much, even to the jaundiced eye of an insurance company.

As he sat eating the rich salad, so full of mayonnaise, egg, bits of ham, and other tasty morsels, and listening with half an ear to the artless chatter of Valya, Felix wondered if this time it was really worth it.

Even with mutual policies of fifteen thousand dollars, he had his doubts. Surely Valya was the worst of the five so far. Valya was grossly fat, and so short as to seem dwarfish. One expected her to proceed by rolling.

Nor did she have that doll-like rosiness that often goes with excess weight. Her complexion was bad, and her eyes, Felix often thought, reminded him of two greatly enlarged flyspecks.

Nothing of his opinion showed on his face, however. Instead, he remarked, with a boyish smile: "The salad is absolutely delicious, dear. You get better every day. And the weather is just perfect for our picnic."

It was much too soon, really, to finish her off, he knew, but the temptation was overwhelming. This was becoming unbearable, even after only six weeks of marriage. Next time he'd try to combine a bit more pleasure with business.

Kathy, his second, in addition to a neat figure, had owned a rather dry wittiness that made for enjoyment. She had lasted over a year, and might still be around except for her large cash surrender value—a life insurance policy worth twelve thousand. That was too much to pay even for wit.

"I'm so glad you like the salad," Valya said, glowing. There was no doubt the creature loved him; but that was nothing remarkable. Six feet of lithe male, deeply tanned, with a little boy grin that blended sex and shyness, had an overpowering appeal.

"One of the family weaknesses," he said, patting her doughy hand. "A lust for the richest food." There was another weakness he didn't mention—murder.

Dear old Dad had pushed his second wife down a flight of stairs. Felix, then a precocious nine, had seen the whole thing from the hall cupboard, where he was lurking. One can't very well blackmail one's own father, but then, on the other hand, Dad had been awfully anxious to please little Felix after that.

And Mother, while a nurse, had quietly, with sound medical efficiency, smothered at least one patient in order to inherit some diamonds left her by the grateful victim. The gems had turned out to be small and flawed, but no doubt Mother had done better on other occasions.

"I suppose every family has its failings and secret vices," Valya said, her thick lips, so smearily made up, working on a sandwich. "We have one ourselves that I've never told a soul about. But now that I'm married—" she gave him a look of shy adoration—"I'll tell you some day."

"Mine isn't secret," Felix grinned, as he gulped a huge éclair. "It's right out in the open. I'm a pig! But I can't see you having any dark secrets; you're a model of rectitude, my dear."

"Oh, we're honest enough. I didn't mean that. And our secret is really nothing so terrible; it's just that people wouldn't understand or approve. In our society, to be different is dangerous. But don't ask me to explain. Later, when we've grown to know each other even better, I wouldn't dream of concealing anything from my darling hubby."

"One more cup of coffee," he said, having lost the thread of her remarks. How the woman did babble at times! "Then I'll be nicely filled. That's good. Thank you, dear."

Yes, he thought, it's risky to dump her today, but what the hell. Nobody has ever come close to suspecting anything. I'll take her to Top of the World for a look at the valley. Then one little push and goodbye to a fat nothing. After that, fifteen thousand and Europe. Paris in the spring, tra la.

"Let me help you clean up," he said, rising in a single graceful movement.

She lurched clumsily to her feet, protesting. "Don't you dare; that's a woman's work." Slowly, awkwardly, she began to gather plastic containers of food, the soiled paper plates, and the crumpled napkins. He could hear her wheezing as she went.

Walking with all the ease of a cow ploughing through a deep snowdrift, she made her slow way to a large wire litter-basket and disposed of the rubbish.

Untidiness, except in her own person, was not a weakness of Valya, Felix mused, watching her with an ironical gleam in his eyes. Funny how somebody so neat in her housekeeping couldn't put on a new, expensive dress without looking like a five-dollar load for the nearest launderette.

"Hurry, dear," he urged. "I want you to see that view from Top of the World before it gets cloudy. Really a magnificent panorama."

"Just one more minute, lambie." She had all the remaining food fitted into the hamper now; a careful, almost mathematical job of packing. "I'm ready," she said. "My, it's so nice we're alone here. Such a lovely spot, and all to ourselves."

"That's because it's only April. By June, there won't be room to spread a napkin, much less a tablecloth. Come on; it's this way."

Arriving at the scenic point—a cliff that overhung the green valley half a mile below—Felix felt his heartbeat quicken. The moment was at hand.

But first, a good look around; nobody must witness this "accident." Luckily, so early in the season and on a weekday, few people could be near. But then, that's how he had hoped it would work out.

"Down there is Lake Calumet," he told her, pointing with a well-manicured finger. "The city, of course, is Fairmount; very plush; a lot of movie stars go there."

He saw her gaze roving eagerly over the superb prospect below, and allowed his own to wander. Not a soul in sight; this was it. He moved up close behind her, putting one hand on a fat shoulder. She leaned back, full of affectionate trust.

"There's another weakness of mine, besides gluttony," he murmured. "I'm afraid it's murder. Goodbye, Valya, dear." And on the last word he gave her a mighty shove, forward over the precipice.

She tipped away under his hand, almost too easily, and without a cry.

Then Felix stood there, frozen in place, his mouth open, his eyes wild, his heart pounding. It was impossible, crazy; a nightmare in broad daylight. Instead of falling, she was just floating there, erect in midair, not two feet from him, her whole body well over the abyss, apparently resting on nothing whatever.

"I was hoping it wouldn't be like this," she said mournfully. "I really loved you, Felix, and prayed that, by a miracle, you might learn to love me. But since it's just money, I'm glad the policy works two ways."

Then her hands were at his collar; they gave one sharp tug, and the green valley swelled up to meet him. A single thin scream came echoing back from the depths as Valya maneuvered herself well over the point, dropping rather heavily to her feet. She peered over the edge of the cliff, shuddered, and shook her head a little sadly.

Valya's secret vice, like that of all her family, was levitation.

The Drum Major

The tenor of his dream changed suddenly. The lovely girl he was pursuing through a sunny garden vanished without a trace. He looked about for her everywhere, feeling deeply frustrated at her disappearance. Only in dreams were young, slim girls at his disposal.

He was preparing to stalk one of her shadowy sisters when he first noticed the darkening sky. A subtle mist, strangely manifest to the eye, settled slowly but relentlessly over the gay, irresponsible world. The sun was obscured, and an oily purple half-light made the cheerful landscape of moments earlier into something strange and sinister.

It was often so, lately. Unsuspecting and happy in the bright amoral Land Beyond Sleep, his youth magically restored, he disported himself, reveling in the godlike powers, the freedom from all restraint, that were his only in dreams. But occasionally, at first, and now too frequently, there occurred at a certain point in his intoxicating Odyssey through the night an abrupt change of mood—the beginning of torment.

All about him the tenuous, subtly deformed creatures of his dream fled like ants before a poison spray; and as they drifted by on soundless feet, all seemed to cry with one voice of fear, "The Drum Major! The Drum Major!"

The Drum Major! Once again he remembered and, remembering, quailed. It came to him with unwelcome clarity that *he* was now the object of pursuit, that from his exalted position of mastery over a whole dream world he had been flung into a gulf of degrading fear. Instead of enforcing his arrogant mandates upon the plastic beings about him, he was in flight, himself, from a nameless pursuer—not merely death—all the more terrifying for being unknown.

As so often before, he would run until his whole body was one flame of muscle agony, and at the last, gasping and sobbing, would draw away from his pursuer to find his home just ahead. He would leap in, barely clear, lock the door, and awake. Wet through with icy sweat, his heart pounding wildly, but awake—oh, the joy of that awakening!—and safe in bed.

He paused irresolutely where he was, wasting precious moments in locating the thing that hunted him. Dazed and sick with sudden fanged memories, he peered about, half-afraid to look directly lest he see too plainly what was best hidden.

There across the smoky, unreal terrain, a huge red shape, hairy, evil in its shambling motion, quartered the dream coverts with fierce eagerness. Its great arms were held aloft, and it bowed itself from side to side as it cast about for his trail.

Frozen in a matrix of fear, the dreamer saw his margin of safety vanishing.

There was still a chance. He would hide. That tree—where had it come from?—with the thick bole. He leaped behind it, and panting, hugged the friendly trunk. For a moment he felt secure, then the bark lost its roughness, becoming smooth and cool. The tree flickered and changed; it was transparent—a thing of glass. And the Drum Major stared ...

The bowed figure rose to stiff erectness, arms flung aloft in triumph; the dreamer's paralysis dissolved, and he whirled to flee.

Behind him a hoarse bellow rang out. The chase was on.

For a few moments the dream-lightness of his feet gave him hope. He leaped with unflinching confidence over ditches, fences, logs, and rivers. He ran effortlessly up obstacle-strewn hills that ascended almost vertically. His feet found paths through apparently impervious tangles of thorny brush, and he cleared with fantastic soaring leaps sky-flung barriers that sprang from nowhere to block his path. Nothing could match his agility; he would race the sun out of the sky; spurn the whole world with his flying feet; he was the god Mercury ...

But the cries of the Drum Major rang again in his ears, and the subtle quicksand that torments the hunted of the Land Beyond Sleep slowed his desperate stride. Every step now meant heart-taxing exertion as he fought his way through meadows of wet grass, deserted streets, cluttered rooms that had never known human inhabitants, long, long corridors lined with doors behind which crouched horrors waiting to spring.

He struggled on, shrieking with fear of imminent hurt, through a vast cellar, black and chill, its damp floor heaped with rusty parts of improbable machinery.

And always just behind, he heard the thudding of splay feet as the Drum Major followed with unfaltering bounds.

The dreamer came to an abrupt decision, one so simple he had overlooked it before. There, just ahead, was a precipitous cliff, the very place from which to plunge, leaving his pursuer cheated on the brink.

He climbed gasping up the rocky slope, dragging each foot with prodigious effort from the clinging muck. At the summit he yelled defiance at the Drum Major, and with a deep breath of exultation hurled himself over. Below, a foaming torrent, black and lusterless, boiled in a narrow gorge.

He fell for hours with nauseating acceleration, and the thin whistle of air past his ears became maddening. But finally the wild river rose to meet him. He knew it well, now. It formed the frontispiece of an edition of *Grimm's Fairy Tales*, a childhood favorite, long forgotten. He braced himself for the icy water.

But somehow, when he landed, he was waist deep in a swamp, and the Drum Major's bubbling cry seared his weary brain.

And then a railroad track appeared before him with a long streamliner, gaily alight, rolling over the rails. He saw the club car, a blaze of color against the lowering sky. It was filled with smartly dressed people, chatting merrily over their drinks, and his heart swelled with longing.

He would be rescued, and join the safe, happy passengers, or he would die beneath the great wheels. He was squarely on the track, daring the enormous black steamer to run him down.

But the train ground to a stop with the grim, old-fashioned steel cowcatcher an inch from his face; every light flashed out, and in vain he ran up and down hammering at the dark cars screaming, "Help! Let me in! Please, please—for the love of God!" There was no response except the sullen drip of oil, the faint hiss of escaping steam, and the sardonic chuckle of a valve.

Again the relentless beat of clawed pads, strangely rhythmic: Lubb-DUPP! Lubb-DUPP! and abandoning his futile pleas, he set off once more, scarcely noting as in mocking irony the train, now brilliantly illuminated, puffed on its carefree way to the world of security and light.

Somewhere deep in his brain an ominous voice chanted a meaningless phrase like an echo to the Drum Major's bounds. "Systole! Diastole! Systole! Diastole!" something jeered as the dreamer fled on his aimless course.

He had reached the uttermost limit of his endurance, and at that moment, as always, his home flashed into view, cheerful and friendly, a refuge within its sturdy brick walls.

He staggered up the porch stairs with the Drum Major breathing hoarsely just behind him. A scaly paw brushed his bare neck as it ripped the collar of his shirt, and the chill contact plucked his deepest heartstring of panic. Then the door slammed to cut off his nemesis, and he was lurching down the long, dim corridor to his room. Again a heavy door was closed and locked behind him, as, weeping with exhaustion, he flung himself upon the bed and lay still.

Never before had he escaped by such a narrow margin, and as he lay there sobbing quietly and framing incoherent phrases of gratitude, a gradual dislimning and refocusing of the room revealed familiar objects in the dawn of a fine spring morning. He was damp with perspiration; his heart throbbed jarringly, but the finches chirped outside in the garden, and he was awake—safe.

As he realized this, a wave of relief, excruciating in its intensity, swept over him, and he stretched luxuriously in the tangled bedclothes.

"That damned greasy food last night," he muttered. "I'm not supposed to eat—" He went rigid in horrified disbelief. What was that heavy tread in the hall?

Something was moving down the corridor toward the bedroom, and his heart beat in time to those steps that made the floor creak.

Then there was a crash as the massive door split down the center like wet cardboard. A hairy arm, stranded with wire-distinct muscles, thrust savagely through the splintered panel, groping, groping …

He closed his eyes. The drumming of his heart swelled to a mad crescendo. Crouching beneath the covers, numb with fright, he sensed but could not see the Drum Major's leap that brought its bulk full upon his heaving chest.

With that intolerable contact, uncouth and furry, the tom-tom of his heart ceased as if a conductor had waved an authoritative baton. For one endless moment he felt the thing crouching on his breast, its warm, foul breath offending his nostrils.

From this second dream, which so falsely had seemed to bring a monster into the real world, he was not destined to escape. Two gulfs, one black and cold, the other crimson and warm, surged toward him in silent contest. He realized, too late, what was on his chest, and the knowledge came just as the blackness won out, dropping him into a night without end.

They found him that morning. Upon his chest, paws neatly folded, and purring gently, Belshazzar, the big Persian, dozed in the warm sunlight that bathed his master's twisted face.

The diagnosis was coronary thrombosis—a fatal heart attack.

The Crime

After three years it was the first day all over again. He looked at the rows of bent heads as the students worked at the final exam. Two of the girls in front had long legs, slim and provocative; their skirts were hiked quite high, and the bare flesh gleamed above short socks. Once he might have thought they exposed themselves deliberately, for his benefit; now he knew it was merely careless preoccupation with the questions. If he had been one of the boys from State, there would have been no such indifference to his reaction.

Heads—brown, blonde, black—and that one magnificent crown of auburn red, the most lovely of all.

A girl glanced up from the paper, and caught his eye. He shrank a little at her cool, impersonal stare. After three years—God knows how many days in class—he still wasn't used to it. Always the same, right from that first terrible day. He recalled an observation from Twain's *Connecticut Yankee* about how the nobility regarded the classless upstart. They admired him, and envied his power, as they might that of an elephant, but could not consider him their equal.

Well, he was not even as good as an elephant here at Rockhurst College; the girls didn't admire him in the least. How could they after losing that suave, witty, and polished professor from Harvard, now in Washington? George Milburn Bracebridge, Ph.D., Mathematics—a top man in numerical analysis, with a family that went back generations here and in England. How could Joe Polanski, M.S. from Illinois Technical College, whose parents hardly spoke English, replace such a man?

It wasn't as if he were a good mathematician, himself. A lousy master's degree that just barely put him ahead of the brighter girls. In normal times this college would not have hired him as a janitor. But now, with so many of their best men in the army, Joe Polanski was a godsend. If it had been simple-minded of him to write the Dean, this was one case where such naivete had paid off. When they learned of his discharge from the army—nothing as romantic as a war wound; he'd never been in combat—for severe asthma, they'd jumped at the chance to hire him for a year or two until their regular faculty came back.

But it was the students' attitude that hurt most. On the first day, tense and sweating, he'd tackled a simple problem in analytic geometry at the board, solving it by an absurdly complicated algebraic approach. When nearly done, he heard snickering and whisperings among the girls, and finally one of them remarked, with the obvious hope of being overheard: "I wonder why he's doing it the hard way—to show us how good he is?"

He had felt himself flushing; then came the sickening realization that his problem, after only a few pages of text, was meant to be solved by the most simple application of mid-points. A matter of two or three minutes, and he had waded through a mile of complicated algebra using the distance formula instead. No wonder they questioned his motives.

"I'm sorry," he stammered. "I just didn't see the easy way. It h-happens sometimes."

As he spoke, he knew he had forgot to modulate his voice; that the nasal harshness was more strident than ever.

Then, later that week, he had been foolish enough to try to demonstrate his sincerity and helpfulness by asking each of them to write, anonymously, on a slip of paper, her suggestions for conducting the class to the best advantage, and—height of folly, this—even personal criticisms. The comments had been wholly merciless, even when meant to be kindly.

"Speak more slowly, and not in a monotone."

"Don't wear beige slacks with a grey jacket."

"Must you sniffle so much?"

The trouble was, he supposed, that they all came from the most exclusive families in the state. Rockhurst was a small and highly selective college, with a student body that even in wartime was never allowed to number more than eight hundred. Although the girls dressed in what seemed to his inexpert eye a kind of casual sloppiness, he guessed that those tweedy skirts and fuzzy sweaters cost more than both of his "good" suits.

At times he thought it was primarily an age difference; they were still in their teens; he was almost thirty. Then he realized it was more of a cultural gap. These girls, with their scrubbed faces, expensive clothes, their perfectly modulated voices and graceful, self-assured bearing, had never known a moment of doubt about their status in society. Oh, they might occasionally agonize over some personal problem—a stolen boyfriend, an outbreak of pimples, a realignment of loyalties by which a cherished friendship was lost, or a bid from the wrong sorority—but he could see in their candid gazes, their easy poise in class, that their white-Anglo-Saxon-Protestant standing was beyond criticism. They need never be ashamed of their parents; hell, their parents ran the state, the college, and most of the big businesses as well.

No, he couldn't really blame them for finding him a bit ridiculous. A squat, dark man, who never looked well-shaved, thanks to a black and wiry beard; somebody with no knack for wearing clothes, even if he ever learned how to buy them; a teacher of mediocre qualifications whose lectures, for what they were worth, were spoiled by an unpleasant voice—one of the girls on her slip had written something poisonous about his "Brooklyn" accent. Of course, he'd been born in Illinois, but to their critical ears, all vulgar accents were "foreign" at worst; "Brooklyn" at best. Their boy friends from State, when they visited the campus, spoke as he would have liked to—in the round, mellow tones of a Robert Taylor or Chet Huntley.

One of the girls was ready to leave; he might have known it. Karen Nilson, the exchange student from Sweden. God, she was bright, and that continental training! She gave him a casual glance from her pale blue eyes as she dropped the paper on his desk. He knew that she despised him, from that day when she'd solved the problem using advanced vector methods. His own knowledge of the subject was shaky at best, but she used the symbols as easily as he did those of elementary algebra. It had been quite clear to the class that he was completely unable to criticize, or even follow, her demonstration. He had restored to the feeble suggestion that she didn't belong in the class and should go ahead to advanced calculus, but there was the usual difficulty about credits and transfer, so there she remained, a student who knew the subject better than her instructor. There was no doubt she helped most of the others with their work, so that they had little interest in his carefully prepared lectures. A number of them quietly read paperback novels on their required lists in English.

When Karen had gone, he picked up her paper. There was hardly any point in going over it; the thing was sure to be perfect.

His eye returned moodily to the auburn hair. The only girl in three years who'd been at all friendly. Laurie Vail. The face under that beautiful halo of red-gold was not really pretty, but the mouth was wide and generous, the nose impish, and the eyes of soft grey-blue like wood-smoke. Not the chilly blue of Karen's.

Laurie was the only one to stop by his office in three years. How many times? Five—just five—ostensibly to ask about problems, but in a subtle, indirect way also to ask him about himself. Gradually he'd told her something about his background, and she listened with apparent sympathy. Not that she was herself lonely or unpopular; nothing like that. Laurie was much sought after as a date, and rightly so; the girl had warmth and vivacity.

And once she'd become rather ill in class. He recalled how he'd asked her what it was, and the evasive answer. Then it occurred to him that it must have been her monthly—what a slow-witted ass he'd been, not to see that without questioning the poor kid. Well, he'd helped her across the campus to her dorm, and the weight of her leaning on his arm was the nicest—in fact, the only nice—memory he would take away from this place. For he was going away. Professor Bracebridge was back; the war was over; and Joe Polanski was out of a job. But that didn't matter; he'd stayed here in spite of his misery because with the prestige of three years at Rockhurst behind him, his chances for a job back in Illinois would be excellent. Even if he didn't get a Ph.D.

Other girls were leaving now; one or two said coolly: "Goodbye, Mr. Polanski," and gave him wintry little smiles. The only reason for these farewells, he thought wryly, was their pleasure in rolling the name across their tongues; it had a sharp foreign flavor, like imported sausage.

He took the papers to the back of the room, and began the work of grading them. It was very easy compared to what the English and Social Science instructors faced. He could glance at the answer, and if it was right, put down a "10." If it was wrong, a hasty survey of the steps would tell him whether the error was a serious one, caused by lack of theory, or the type due to haste in arithmetic. The latter meant only a point or two off.

As he worked, the room gradually emptied; the girls now left their papers on the front desk, and had no reason to say goodbye.

When he looked up, blinking, half an hour later, only one girl was left. There was no mistaking the auburn head. Laurie was just sitting there, her hands on the desk, her paper to one side. As he watched, a sunbeam brought life to the reddish tendrils, and the whole mass shone with highlights. He stared, fascinated by the color and warmth of it. The girl sighed—a deep inspiration almost like a moan—and put her head back.

So they were alone, the two of them. Surely it hadn't just happened. Laurie meant it to happen. Now she sat there, head back against the seat, waiting for him to—to do what? What did he want to do? Nobody would come by; the dorms were at the far end; the gym closed for this term. Certainly he could take her in his arms, at least; there were so many things to tell her. But first, above all, that glorious hair. There was something peculiarly Polish about auburn hair of that darkly shining kind. His mother, as a girl, must have had hair like that.

Hardly aware of what he was doing, he slipped out of his seat and moved very quietly up behind her. Noiselessly he eased himself into the seat just behind the girl, and studied her hair. It was held in place by bobby pins; he could see the bluish curved tops buried in the reddish mass. He leaned closer, and caught the faint scent of some spicy perfume, not the sexy kind, he thought vaguely; the spring violet type connecting youth, gaiety, innocence.

Without his volition, his hand reached up to tug at one of the pins. He pulled it out; she didn't move; but a single strand fell free, shining in the sunbeam. Hastily he removed others; soon her hair was a bronze cataract flowing over his chunky dark hands.

"Oh, Laurie," he said, burying his fingers in the springy coils. "Oh, Laurie, Laurie."

Her head dropped to one side; a sudden chill drove deep into his bones. He sprang up, badly wrenching one knee, and then stretched over and around the seat. The wood-smoke eyes were fixed and glassy; the girl's chest didn't move.

The door opened, and Karen stood there.

"I forgot my notebook—" she began; then he saw her eyes widen, her mouth go oddly slack. She gave him a single startled glance, then whirled out of the room.

"Miss Nilson!" he called after her, but it was too late. Too late for anything now; certainly too late to put the girl's hair back in place. He was trying it, with thick, clumsy fingers, when the Dean and a nurse came in.

"I f-found her like that," he explained.

The Dean looked at the dead girl's hair streaming over the back of the chair, and his mouth tightened to a pursy blue knot.

"Her hair," Polanski said. "I didn't mean—you see—"

"Never mind," the Dean said. "Later, Mr. Polanski. Later."

When he left the campus two days later, never to return, he passed a small group of girls by the dorm.

One voice came clearly to his ears; it was sweet, mellow, and pure. It was a poisoned barb.

"Imagine," the voice sang. "To do that after she was dead."

A Letter from Réjane

"I faltered only once in my desire to be an actress," Madame D'Anjou said, her famous organ voice dominating all the others.

There was a polite murmur of dismay at the loss that might have been incurred by the stage. In spite of a promising field of young newcomers, Madame D'Anjou was still the grande dame of the theatre, an aging empress with no serious rivals. Without her, Broadway would be like a kingdom lacking its anointed ruler.

"They say you made up your mind while practically a child," Diana Travers said, her clipped tones an odd contrast to those of the older actress. "After seeing something quite juvenile—was it 'Peter Pan'?"

"Exactly right, darling. I was just eleven, and the moment Wendy spoke her first lines, I said to my mother: 'Some day *I* shall be Wendy.' And mother laughed—she had the most delicious gurgle."

"You had the last laugh," Barry Carruthers said. "You must have played that part hundreds of times. I understand they literally had to cast you as Peter because nobody cared to compete with your remarkable Wendy."

"You're much too flattering, Barry, darling. But there's a grain of truth in the story for all that. I did do a rather nice Wendy. And Barrie was surefire theatre in those days."

"But what about your nearly abandoning the stage?" Eleanor Tremayne demanded. "In all the years I've known you, that's news to me. I could have sworn you never deviated by a hair after playing Wendy."

"I'd quite forgotten the incident," Madame D'Anjou said placidly. "Until just now. Odd, how bits and pieces of one's past pop up at random that way. Like old film-clips of the mind, almost."

"We must hear the story," Diana said. "If you had chosen a different career, some of us might have had better luck!"

"Very well. As if anything could have stopped me from telling about it! Age makes one quite anecdotal."

"You are perfectly timeless," Barry said. "Not a tiny change even, in the fifteen years I've known you, Solange."

"He makes it sound quite believable, the rogue," Madame D'Anjou said, her voice creamier than ever. "Always fish for compliments from a professional mime—you end up being convinced in spite of yourself. It helps the ego no end. But, Barry, darling, we're among old friends. Everybody here knows I'll never see sixty again."

"According to 'Who's Who'," one woman whispered to her escort, "she's seventy-eight. But I will say she doesn't look it, not by a dozen years."

"Dear Madame D'Anjou—the story, if you please," Diana said.

"Of course, my dear. But you mustn't expect anything earthshaking. It was like a pebble in the road, a small thing, but enough to deflect quite a heavy vehicle at the right moment. Patience; I begin.

"It was a long time ago, in the year—but no dates. I had just begun my stage career for a second time, so to speak. One succeeds as a child; then comes the age of long legs and awkwardness. After playing Barrie while still a baby, it was humiliating to find myself in bit parts as a young woman. Servant girls, Maids of Honor in costume dramas—you know the types. Meanwhile I burned to do Nora in 'A Doll's House', or Candida. They were what I really wanted and thought myself ready for, naturally. What young actress doesn't feel that way?

"Then I went to see the great Réjane. None of you infants would remember her, but she was—who can describe such a woman, such an actress? There's nobody like her today. You might as well look for another Shaw, or a novelist with the great, gusty drive of Dickens. Ours is a puny generation by comparison. Réjane was power, magic, flawless technique, stage presence, sensuous beauty—a deep femininity Hollywood cannot counterfeit. And her voice—one moment silver bells, little tinkling bells, and the next the harsh, raging notes of a grieving Hecuba. But no amount of heaped adjectives can set her before you; you must take my word for it.

"Well, I saw her. I was just seventeen. The play? It would make you laugh today. One of those absurd melodramas so popular in the Eighties. Possibly by Sardou—or was it Henry Arthur Jones? To think he was so famous then, and now I can't remember the order of his names. Henry Arthur, or Arthur Henry. A contemporary of Shaw, actually, and forgotten, quite.

"Anyway, it was the kind of play that would be hooted out of a small town in Arkansas, or the provinces of France, today. But Réjane—she could recite the telephone directory and make you weep. Her big scene was some business with a letter. She was writing it to her lover, the man who had betrayed her. You smile, but we cried. It was the spirit of the times, partly, but Réjane above all. She wrote the letter, and as she put down those words—those pathetic words written from her heart's blood—she read them aloud. The stage was empty, except for her, you understand. No playwright today would dare use such a device. But in the Eighties it was *de rigueur*; after all, the audience had to know the contents. In the same way, there were those endless soliloquies, all designed to keep the listeners informed. Nobody thought of doing it in a more natural subtle way by dialogue. Until Ibsen swept all that aside. Today only Shakespeare is permitted a soliloquy.

"But Réjane, she read the letter aloud, her cheeks wet with tears, her pen moving in rhythm with the words. I watched her in awe, admiration, and despair—yes, despair. The woman was tearing herself apart emotionally over that letter, living every phrase. It came to me then, as I looked on, that the stage was not for me. It was not possible,

I knew, for me to experience such emotions without a critical drain on my body's vitality. I thought back to my airy roles as Peter or Wendy, when the imminent death of Tinker Bell called for a few moments of bald grief, and felt scalding shame at my past inadequacy.

"But then it occurred to me that perhaps Réjane didn't do this at every performance. Surely nobody could without breaking down. Maybe tonight was something special. I had to know.

"As a member of the profession, I had my little privileges. One of them was a ready entrée backstage in most theatres. So I went to see Réjane directly the curtain fell.

"She was very gracious; Réjane could never be otherwise. Her spirit was as beautiful as her acting. Although she was tired and warm, and wanted her bath badly, she was willing to give a few moments to a novice like me. Her warmth and quick comprehension quickly led me to confide in her. When I spoke of the letter scene, and my self-doubt, she laughed—I can still hear that full voiced golden mirth of Réjane's.

"'You poor silly little goose!' she said, and there was no offence in her words. 'Would you like to see the famous letter? Let me show you what I was actually writing; the boy will be here to post it in a moment.'

"She reached into her bodice, and took out the folded bit of paper, all warm and scented from her body. I read it uncomprehendingly at first. It was a casual invitation to some friends of hers. I can still quote it verbatim:

My dear Jean and Marie:

Wednesday will be ideal, I think, for our little supper together. I do hope you are free. Because of the matinee, there will be no evening performance, so I can relax and enjoy both of you. Give my love to your grandpapa.

"You see the point, darlings. Réjane was spouting all that pathos with her thoughts elsewhere—but completely withdrawn. She told me she often took care of any last minute business or social correspondence right there on stage, with hundreds of people admiring her reading of the letter. All of you know the secret. After playing a part for many months, one goes through the whole thing quite mechanically. And yet—it's more than that. It's as if one half of you, the better, professional half, does the acting while the rest of you moves aside. The audience is not cheated; it's just that there is no other way to keep such a role alive for so long a run. Am I not right?

"Well, after that, I never doubted myself or faltered again. The stage was my life, and still is. You have often flattered me. You and the critics, bless them.

"Ah, but you should have seen Réjane …"

Birthday in a Garden

It was pleasantly cool in the garden, although the morning had been quite warm. The flowerbeds were masses of color, and the late afternoon light had that short-lived clarity that seems to come only at certain rare moments, when sun and air, temperature and shade, are all perfectly mated. It was a unique moment in time and space, prelude to a unique moment in two lives.

In that almost crystal transparency Patricia suddenly saw Barry's face as if in a magnifying mirror. Each little nest of humorous wrinkles at the corners of his eyes was highlighted. Odd that she'd never noticed before how deep and numerous they were. And the grey at his temples; ordinarily it was hardly visible; now the oblique rays of the sun, and some trick of the atmosphere, emphasized that first subtle frost of age. Only the youthfulness of Barry's spirit, and her own blindness, could have so long obscured the facts. Maybe the whole world, and everything in it, had a new aspect, amounting to a revelation, on this, her twentieth birthday.

"Pat," he said, a faint note of wonder in his voice, "I won't offer a mere penny for your thoughts in these days of inflation, but you do have a most peculiar look in your eyes. I thought I knew all your moods, but this is something different. One of those fey Scots expressions people talk about. Might I ask what it means? What were you thinking just then?"

"I'm not sure I was thinking at all," she said, uneasily aware of her evasion. "Just feeling—taking the world in through my skin. A new world today, somehow. But if I thought of anything that can be put into words, it was how distinguished you suddenly look in this light. The clear air seems to bring it out. It's as if I'd never seen you at all before; only photos or sketches."

For just a moment his hand came down lightly on her bare shoulder. She was very conscious of that brief touch. Without seeing it, she visualized his hand, sinewy, rather square; capable of the most precise work on the piano or in bandaging a bird's broken wing. It was seldom that Barry attempted any physical contact with her. He had always forced his attention on her mind. No, that wasn't quite fair, either. There had been no imposition of ideas. Instead he had tended her intellect as he would a frail shoot in the garden, destroying nearby weeds, supplying good nourishment, and allowing the organism its own unique flowering. If the young plant was maturing into something strong and beautiful, all honor to the gardener.

"In this air, or any air, you're a very lovely girl, Pat. It's wonderful, isn't it, to be twenty and beautiful?"

"I won't be modest, not today. Yes, it's wonderful."

"I've known you for twenty years today—your whole life."

"I've known you just as long," she smiled, her hazel eyes meeting his own ironic blue ones steadily. "That makes us even."

"Hardly. I watched you grow up; even had a hand in it. That gives me an edge." There was laughter behind his words, but something more on his face.

A hummingbird hovered before them, its wings blurred, body motionless against the sky. Too fast for the eye to follow it veered sideways to explore a honeysuckle plant.

"They're so alive," Pat said. "I don't know of anything else that seems to live so intensely."

"Because their lives are short. If you were a hummingbird, you'd want to make every moment count, too."

"I do anyhow!" she cried, throwing her arms wide.

"But that's only because you're twenty."

"You say that almost enviously. Yet you've told me a thousand times that you'd hate to be a boy again."

"It's true—at least, it was true. There are no miseries like those of the young. They suffer terribly over things that later will seem completely trivial. But the suffering is real; no adult ever has such pangs again. Bad ones, but not the same species at all. Yet there are compensations. Happiness at twenty is the kind of ecstasy that won't return at forty. And, of course, two young people—" He broke off, as if in fear of betraying himself.

They were near a bench. Wordlessly they sat down together. The clear light was dimming; the air became suddenly chill. The scent of jasmine overpowered the daytime flowers. Pat shivered slightly.

His hand touched her shoulder again, lingered there.

"You must know what I'm thinking," he murmured. "You always do."

She hesitated, then replied: "I won't pretend. You did teach me to be perceptive—and honest. And I know the way your mind works. Yes, Barry, I can guess what you're thinking. It began a little while ago when the light was so clear, almost like magic here in the garden."

"How do you feel about me, then? As a friend of the family? As your own special friend? A sort of uncle, perhaps?"

"As all of those. And more—so much more. I've learned so many fine things from you. Music, art, literature—but that sounds so dreary and academic. They weren't really learned; they were absorbed— drunk like sparkling wine. You taught me how to live fully, without fear, like that hummingbird. How to become mature; how to be myself and to live with myself. Things my parents, with all their love, couldn't give me. Those teenage miseries you just mentioned; I've seen all my friends go through them. But thanks to you, I've managed to avoid the worst ones. It's been easy growing up this way."

"Then it's gratitude." There was no reproach in his voice.

She was silent.

"I love you," he said. "You know that. We understand each other. We enjoy the same things. I think I could make you happy."

"You always have. In a way I do love you. But, Barry, I'm twenty. This is my twentieth spring. It's your fiftieth."

"And that matters a great deal to you."

"Not in the way you think. You're a very attractive man. I'm sure you know it; plenty of women must have made it plain. I've seen some of them myself. From the time I was twelve, I haven't missed much about you. If I were interested in an affair, you'd be ideal. For that matter, as a husband you'd be wonderful. I've learned a lot from you, and I'll put it to good use. I know just what to look for in a man. I won't fall for the first pretty boy with muscles, like some of my friends have done—to their regret. I'll find a boy with kindness, with your kind of perception, your love of music. I don't mean he'll be another Barry, not at twenty-five. But he'll have the potential. At fifty, I hope he'll be very much like you.

"But, Barry, dear, don't hate me for what I must say. I need to find those qualities in somebody of my own generation. Somebody I can grow old with. One of the best things you taught me was not to be afraid to grow old; that age has its own beauty and power. And we'll have to make our own mistakes, that boy and I. We won't make bad ones, thanks again to you. But it needs a few mistakes to bring people together, too. Do you understand me?" She didn't wait for his answer, but laughed a bit shakily. "What a foolish question, when I learned understanding from you."

He was silent for a moment. Then he said in a low voice: "You're right, of course. It was foolish of me to expect anything else. You'll find what you want; what I've taught you to need; what you deserve. And you'll find it in somebody the right age. Somebody who still remembers his twentieth birthday. To be honest, I can't. But I'd have been a bigger fool if I let you go without asking."

In the dusk she could barely see his face, but she kissed him on the mouth, and for a moment her hand touched his cheek. Then he was alone on the bench.

The Odyssey of Epeira

Shining blue and silver in the bright sun, and heady from its rays, a great bluebottle fly whirled in mad curves about the quiet garden. For all the handsome insect's gallant coloring, a powerful microscope would have brought into startling focus the horror of its hairy legs, alive with the germs of a dozen terrible diseases.

As its superb wings, beating the air more than three hundred times each second, swept it in a widening arc, the insect smashed squarely against a tough, sticky network of silvery threads.

A single long buzz of fear, easily distinguished from the preceding ones by a sudden rise in pitch, rang thinly, futilely over the flowers. Fighting wildly against the almost invisible restraint, the big fly became hopelessly entangled as the spirally-wound threads stretched to double their original length without snapping. The blurred wings were gripped and held immobile by the elastic strands; the victim buzzed once more—a plaintive, pitiful sound—and then a fearful apparition: Epeira!

From the center of the web, where all vibrations converged on a little cushion of silk, there led a single thick strand. Up, away from the web, connected to it only at the center, this thread ran to a hole between the bricks some four inches higher, where in the cool dusk, Epeira the spider, crouched with the sensitive tip of one hind leg just touching her primitive telegraph wire.

As the signal thread vibrated to the desperate struggles of the heavy bluebottle, tickling Epeira's clawed foot, she awoke to instant savage life, seeming to flow towards the web, so smooth her motion. As she emerged from the dark, silk-lined tunnel, there was a single instant when the sun struck her eyes at just the right angle to transform them into a pattern of glittering jewels.

Out upon the sticky web, which insects, lacking the protective oil of a spider's feet, cannot cross, she made her effortless way, to pause briefly short of her prey and survey it with eyes blank and soulless. There was little need for caution, however. Completely contemptuous of the unarmed victim, possessing neither fangs nor sting, she closed in with a ferocious little rush.

Again a shrill buzz. Instinct, if nothing else, told the fly that here was the arch enemy of its race—the eight legged monster which, if flies dream, must stalk through their most frightful nightmares.

Ignoring the pathetic plaint, Epeira calmly swathed the fly in silk from her spinning glands, and soon the victim was a mere helplessly vibrating bundle, clad veritably in a shroud. Dragging the bluebottle by a single thread, Epeira returned to her gloomy lair, there to consume the fly at leisure.

Later in the day the fierce huntress cast the drained body of her prey to the ground beneath the web, and set about repairing the damaged snare. While she was patching the last small rent, Fate, proving more than usually generous this afternoon, sent her another catch.

It was a terrifying insect, some three inches tall, with a pointed, evilly-inquisitive head that pivoted from side to side in a motion that was almost human. Of all insects this one alone can direct its basilisk gaze in such a fashion.

Its long green-lace wings were hopelessly caught by the relentless threads, but the powerful jointed forearms with their keen spines were both free and eager. Let the fragile spider venture but once within their grasp, and the dagger-filled shears formed by the elbow-joints would quickly crush out her life. The praying mantis is not a common victim of Epeira's snare; it prowls the grass-roots jungle, and is more often the hunter than the hunted.

This particular mantis had already proved its fitness as a warrior. Earlier in the day, while devouring a foolish green grasshopper, it had stopped mumbling the victim just in time to defend itself against a deadly foe from above.

Rocking on blurred wings directly over its head, a hunting wasp had marked the mantis for her prey. The wasp's womb teemed with eggs, and her life work was the procurement of a paralyzed mantis for each one of her offspring.

Once successful in confusing the mantis long enough to alight on its back, the wasp had a remarkable technique for mastering the giant. Her jaws would grip the slender neck, and as her six legs twined hastily about the surprised creature, her abdomen, bearing the unsheathed sting, would curl forward and under to plunge the dagger deep into the nerve center controlling the mantis' formidable weapons. Then, as the spiked forelegs dropped numbly to the victim's sides, the wasp would slide down her foe's back as a man goes down a pole, her stiletto again ready. On reaching a position opposite the middle pair of legs, she would strike home once more, and moving still lower, finish the job by paralyzing the two legs remaining.

But not always is the wasp victorious in the grim combat. This time her trick failed, and before she could withdraw, the great mantis had caught her slender body in its cruel arms, piercing her through.

Why, after its unusual victory, the mantis had laboriously dragged its clumsy body up the old brick wall is a mystery locked in the creature's minute brain. In any case, the action doomed the mantis, for a crumbling bit of mortar dropped the insect squarely in Epeira's web.

It was a spectral sight, struggling there, begging the spider to come within reach, but Epeira was not daunted. Outweighed and out-armed by her catch, there was nevertheless something about her hairy body with its puffy abdomen that made her a more fearful sight than even the huge mantis.

Little by little Epeira edged closer to the monster, pausing after each brief advance to measure the mantis with flat, empty eyes, lidless and jewel-bright. No panicky buzzing here. The mighty insect strained to reach the spider, and the spiny traps opened and closed with fierce anticipation.

It was not to be, however. Epeira had a much better way. Not by risking her slight body—a pea on eight slender legs—does the garden spider triumph. Instead, with the contemptuous air of one holding all the trumps, she turned about and began to spin silk. Not the mere threads which had sufficed for the despised bluebottle, but great sheets and gobs streamed from her glands. From a point just beyond reach of the raging mantis, using her rearmost pair of legs, she flung huge swathes of the sticky material over her writhing captive.

It was soon over. Tangled and almost smothered by the inexorable rain of silk, its murderous shears completely immobile, the mantis never had a chance for the single combat it sought. It was Retiarius versus Secutor: net and trident against sword, as it might have been fought a million years before Rome, with the net-caster triumphant. Too heavy to be dragged away, the mantis died there beneath the poison fangs it was powerless to resist.

But Epeira was not destined to profit from this particular victim, the first of its kind she had encountered. A stick in the hands of a child ripped the wonder of her web to tatters and flung Epeira herself several feet away into the tangled brush. The icy assurance of the huntress vanished instantly. The queen of death in her web, she became a blindly frantic fugitive away from it. She scuttled wildly through the grass-stems, first one way, then another. A butterfly, easiest of prey in her snare, caused Epeira to crouch in needless apprehension, and the whining zoom of a fly froze her in place as if she had never before heard that familiar dinner-bell sound.

After surviving a few such scares, Epeira recovered some of her poise, but still proceeded with caution. She was about to return home, when a tragedy occurred not ten inches from her. Two marauding gold beetles, incredibly ferocious slayers, arrogant in their brilliant armor, charged into a little group of meek caterpillars. Panic-stricken, the victims separated with rippling haste, but the beetles were like wolves worrying sheep as they went mad with the lust to kill. They wreaked butcher-like carnage with their keen mandibles, never pausing until every caterpillar was torn to bits.

Epeira fled, utterly horrified by the blind ferocity of the beetles. For almost an hour she ran aimlessly through the sun-drenched grass, and when she finally stopped, exhausted, she had lost all sense of direction.

Suddenly she felt a sharp pain in one leg, and discovered that a tiny red ant had fastened to her with all the bulldog persistence of its tribe. It was quickly joined by two others, but Epeira dragged all three with her as if they were weightless, so overwhelming was her fright. She had blundered into a nest which was now boiling over. By some mysterious signal the red raiders had been alerted. A dozen gnawed at her and despite her most desperate resistance pulled her ever backwards toward the black mouth of the nest. Once forced crumpled and dying down that lightless shaft, Epeira would be seen above ground no more. Her furiously clashing fangs, too big for her need, closed harmlessly about the tiny attackers or slipped from their tough, smooth armor. The nest marked by a collar of fine yellow sand was very near now.

But it was not Epeira's time to die. A large black ant had appeared near the nest, followed soon by others. For many years the two ant tribes had waged incessant and costly warfare. They hated each other with all the venom so characteristic of internecine strife.

No more red ants joined those dragging Epeira. Instead, all closed with the black invaders, gnawing at legs and jaws like scarlet fiends. Nor were the big ants less willing; each left a trail of crippled red warriors in its path.

As for the ants holding Epeira, whenever one relaxed its grip to run about for a breather—a custom peculiar to ants—it invariably met a black ant with which it preferred to battle. As a result, Epeira soon found herself free, and she hastened from the arena without further molestation.

Feeling impelled to seek the heights, the spider climbed easily to the top of a slender green stem surmounted by a nodding bloom. Below her there lay unnoticed a cluster of pitcher-shaped leaves with red veinings. As she paused, uncertain about her next move, the decision was made for her. A clumsy locust ended its erratic flight on the stem, and the resulting jar flipped Epeira so quickly into one of the pitchers directly below, that she was unable to leave the usual lifeline of silk behind her.

To Epeira's horror, she found herself kicking in chilly liquid, and upon attempting to scale the wall, found it lined with stiff hairs, pointing down and effectually blocking ascent.

There was a broken bit of leaf floating in the watery fluid, and Epeira eagerly climbed aboard, there to crouch quietly in the weird light that filtered green-hued through the walls of the insect-eating plant.

She was not left alone for long, however. Something heavy landed on the rim of the pitcher, making the leaf raft rock dangerously in the waves of liquid. Then, with a mighty splash, a great beetle tumbled into the water. Utterly bewildered, it thrashed about with all the strength of its massive body. Several times its wing-covers opened, and it attempted to fly, but unable to go straight up, it ended by striking the side walls and falling back into the water. Twice it overturned the bit of leaf, spilling Epeira, but the raft was far too small to sustain its weight, and before long the beetle floated quietly, motionless except for spasmodic twitchings of its antennae. Here was a platform more stable than the leaf, now waterlogged and sinking. Epeira climbed gratefully upon the insect's shiny back, which swayed gently as she balanced there.

A second visitor paid a brief call. It was a five-inch dragonfly with crisp, iridescent wings and immense, many-faceted eyes. It watched Epeira speculatively, but fearing to risk its stiff, unretractable wings in the depths of the pitcher, flew off with a papery rustle to snatch a mosquito in midair.

The next caller was infinitely more dangerous, because it had some knowledge of pitcher plants. With keen apprehension Epeira saw a mysterious shadow move smoothly up the sunlit side of her prison, which rocked slightly as the climber halted on the rim.

It was a huge wolf spider. Independent of a web and twice the size of Epeira, it was a first-class killing machine, having long been the scourge of the region. In its brief existence it had devoured thousands of insects, mostly flies, but had no prejudice against cannibalism. Now it dispassionately surveyed the prisoners of the pitcher, where it came often for easy prey. Well aware of the treacherous hairy lining, it entered safely by a thick thread of silk, securely fastened to the lip of the pitcher.

Down, smoothly down, the wolf spider came, controlling with great nicety the silk that poured from its spinnerets. It was almost directly over Epeira; she could see its clashing mandibles like magnified images of her own. In a sudden panic Epeira floundered off her beetle raft, and struggling wildly in the water, attempted once more to scramble up the furry walls.

The wolf spider, sure ultimately of its prey, paused only momentarily, and then completed its descent, coming to rest on the beetle. Its fierce yet empty eyes formed a pattern of emerald dots, reflecting the greenish light. What picture those dots conveyed to the tiny brain, man cannot say, but the hunter knew its victim and gathered itself for the lightning spring which in ferocity and boldness is not often matched in the animal kingdom.

Then came upheaval, abrupt and terrifying. The giant, heavily armored beetle was not yet dead. With the incredible vitality of its kind, it went into a grotesque whirlwind of blind, lashing activity—the death flurry of an insect leviathan.

Completely surprised, the wolf spider was tossed into the swirling liquid, and as chance would have it, the madly-clashing jaws of the beetle, powerful enough to draw blood from a man's finger, crushed the head and brain of the floundering killer.

It was the beetle's last struggle. In a few seconds it floated motionless by the sinking body of its victim. Already the plant's fluid had started its slow digestion of both prizes.

Epeira, half drowned, once again scrambled aboard the beetle's body. For many minutes she rested there, gradually recovering her vitality as she dried. The long thick thread, still ironically fastened to the corpse of the wolf spider, glistened silver-green in the subdued light of the setting sun, and something awoke in the white pinpoint that was Epeira's brain.

She struggled up the wolf spider's lifeline, and without hesitating on the pitcher's rim, made her way hurriedly to the ground.

That very night, on another section of the old fence, Epeira began the scaffolding of a bigger and better web.

The Black Tyrant

A dark speck in the sky came swirling down with a peculiar side-slipping motion, revealing itself as a large, black bird. The keen eyes, wiser than a mere bird's rightfully should be, instantly spotted the dead trout—a neat, semi-circular bite taken through its backbone—just as a playful otter had left it there on the beach some moments earlier.

The otter had been full to repletion, but at the irresistible sight of the darting fish had lunged into swift pursuit, overtaking the fleeing creature in three mighty strokes, and nipping it expertly through the spine. Then, not hungry enough even to sample a second bite, the otter had flipped the carcass ashore, and whistling joyfully, rejoined its sleek mate in a wild water frolic.

"R-rark!" cried the raven exultantly, and turning on his back in midair, practiced the terrible slash with pickaxe beak which he had learned from his father a quarter century before.

If there was one thing which characterized the unpredictable black tyrant, it was this same deadly whirl-over-and-slice.

Circling cautiously about the dead fish, Rark inspected every possible covert from which his chief enemy, man, might launch an attack. Twenty-five years earlier, Rark had broken his shell, a fuzzy, ugly chick, and now, in the fullness of age, he was wise beyond most birds.

Rark could count at least to five, and this knowledge had at least once saved his life. A farmer, angry over the raven's barnyard poaching, had laid a cunning trap for him. In plain view of the bird, the farmer had placed some savory scraps upon a tree stump and, armed with a shotgun, had hidden, with four of his family, in a smokehouse nearby.

Knowing himself under observation by the wary raven, the farmer, with three of his companions, then left the shack, all four returning home in a noisy group.

But Rark had counted five entering the smokehouse, and only four leaving—without the shotgun, too—whereupon with a jeering "Arrk! R-rark!" he had flapped upwind to outstay the lone watcher.

After waiting vainly almost an hour, the disgruntled man left, taking good care to remove the food scraps, but in spite of this petty retaliation, Rark rightfully considered himself victor in their battle of wits.

And now, his inspection producing no evidence of a trap, Rark alighted beside the fish, and with a pleased croak began to feast.

He had taken only half a dozen pecks at the firm flesh, however, when his watchful senses warned him of a rival. The challenger was a red fox, which slunk towards Rark wearing that expression of slyness, insolence, and intelligence so typical of Reynard.

Rark hopped reluctantly off the fish, regarding the intruder with warning haughtiness. Was he, Rark, master of the air for miles around, whom even the terrible falcons of Chalk Ledge dared not molest in flight, to be robbed of his prize by a sneaking red rascal? He danced about angrily with half-opened wings, glancing down his wicked beak at the advancing fox.

The newcomer was taken aback by this determined stand by a mere bird, one of a class of feeble—and tasty—creatures that supplied part of his food. He paused momentarily, being far too cautious by nature and experience to plunge headlong into a doubtful situation.

Yet it was only a bird, after all. What if the powerful black wings did span more than a yard? The fox had easily killed geese of greater size. Besides, the ripe odor of the trout was tickling his sensitive nostrils, and fish was a rare dainty. His black lips curled back in a grating snarl as he sprang forward to snap at this bold fowl.

But Rark was no longer there when the keen white fangs clashed together. He knew the power of those narrow, punishing jaws. The raven didn't move very gracefully, but somehow he was out of reach in a surprisingly short time.

The fox looked about with a contemptuous air, wondering where the bird had gone, and finally saw the raven rocking clumsily just out of lunging distance overhead. Reynard felt a little sheepish, but if the black bird was wise enough not to defy him, very well. All he wanted right now was fish. With a single warning snarl he returned to the torn trout.

This fox, however, was still young, and his experience though varied, had not included ravens, since they are no longer common. He had much to learn about the breed in general and Rark in particular. Before his drooling jaws could close over the tempting morsel, there was a single grating "Kr-r-rark!" and the raven alighted squarely on the fox's back. Twice the mighty beak struck the red fur, and at each lightning jab a deeper red stained the animal's body.

With a dog-like yelp of agony the fox rolled over, snapping madly at the painful wounds, but Rark was again flapping safely out of reach, his eyes gleaming with malice.

The fox attempted to lick the deep gashes, and having no success, returned gloomily to his dinner. Instantly Rark, a beak-wielding fury, struck again, doing appalling additional damage to the same bleeding cuts.

It was enough for Reynard. Never before had he met such a diabolical fowl, and no fish was worth continuing the acquaintance. He cast a single scornful glance at the trout as if to imply that such leftovers, although good enough for ravens, were beneath his contempt. Then, vainly trying to preserve the superior air so prized by foxes, he slunk unhappily into the brush.

Croaking contentedly, Rark flopped down to finish his meal. Out of the corner of one eye he watched with satisfaction the disheartened fox's departure. He had pecked at the hound-torn remains of generations of foxes; in fact, he had often followed red-coated huntsmen to be early at the kill. Naturally, therefore, he had little respect for foxes. Truthfully, Rark had little respect for any of his competitors.

As the raven ate, he was surrounded gradually by a group of hopeful, impatient followers: several seagulls, a villainous crow, and two cowardly turkey vultures. All of them knew Rark of old, and although the vultures uttered mewing pleas from time to time, it was not until Rark had fed full and flown heavily away that these lesser pirates dared to squabble over his leavings, which were scanty indeed.

That night there came a terrible gale to cap a month of bitter cold, and as a sickly dawn broke, the subsiding breakers, still turbulent and smoky, left the carcass of a small whale high upon the littered beach.

As the morning light grew slowly in strength, it might have revealed to a keen eye a whitish blob that broke the whale's sleek outline. Closer examination would have identified the blob as a rare visitor to a temperate coast. It was an arctic owl, a giant of its kind, and although badly buffeted by the storm that had swept it far off-course, it appeared formidable enough, hunched there quietly atop the whale with fierce, yellow eyes staring unblinkingly at nothing.

For hours the mighty predator rested immobile upon the whale, as the dying storm blew itself out and a feeble orange sun tinted the deserted beach. Slowly the owl was regaining the vitality beaten from its body by the violent and icy winds it had fought through the night.

Once a tiny water vole poked its whiskered face from a hole beneath a piece of driftwood to look longingly at the whale's great bulk; but some subtle sense apparently warned it, for with a single terrified glance at the motionless white figure, it scurried to the very bottom of the tunnel, there to crouch hungry but safe in its grass-lined nest.

In the late afternoon another visitor of a sterner caliber appeared. Like a twisting steel spring in motion, this fearless mite—a tiny ermine, whose six-inch body confined the implacable fighting spirit of the fiercest lion—bounded confidently toward the stranded whale.

A long scar, almost hidden beneath the silky fur, testified to this ermine's courage. Some days before, a large sparrow hawk, more rash than wise, had seized the white weasel and carried it aloft. To the hawk's dismay the tiny creature had twisted like a mass of compressed springs to nip the scaly legs ten times in three seconds. The agonized bird had promptly dropped its prey, and except for superficial talon wounds, the weasel was unharmed, falling to the thick grass as lightly as an insect.

Although the fierce hunter preferred fresh food—blood above all—the spell of frigid weather had made hunting difficult, and cold blubber was better than nothing.

So the weasel, with ruddy, hunger-bright eyes in a triangular mask of fury, made its loping way toward a huge flipper and failed to observe the owl slowly turning its head until its great brooding eyes glared directly at the ermine.

Silently, like a puff of white smoke, the bird of prey launched its six pounds of assassin's equipment into the frosty air. Its flight feathers, edged with the softest down, made no whisper of that sound which accompanies the wing-beats of most other birds, and the weasel had no warning whatever.

Knife-like talons met in its body; the raging jaws gnashed harmlessly against the thickly feathered legs; its dauntless heart beat a dozen times, and the grim spirit flickered out.

A moment later the white owl, perched again upon the whale, was tearing hungrily at the tough flesh of the weasel's body. That the meat was unbearably rank meant little to the eater, for its sense of taste, like that of most owls, was rudimentary.

The owl had just gulped the last sour morsel, when a large, black bird flapped heavily towards the cove. It was Rark, hungry and ill tempered after a bad night on a windswept perch.

More observant than the reckless weasel, he spotted the great owl immediately, but never having met one before, circled about, inspecting the white invader. He carefully noted the impressive bulk, the potent beak, and the haughty carriage, but was not awed. No doubt this was merely a new kind of buzzard, whose hooked beak meant little without a fighting heart. It couldn't be a falcon, a bird Rark knew and respected; falcons didn't sit like that—they dived upon their prey and were gone. Because of the white plumage, barred with brown,

Rark recognized nothing owl-like. He had met the great horned owl at sunset on occasion, and gave it a wide berth, especially after he had seen it carry off a full-grown tomcat one summer evening. But who ever heard of a white owl, and sitting in the open by day?

No, there was little need for caution, and alighting ungracefully upon the dead whale, Rark cocked his head in the direction of the stranger. He was accustomed to a certain amount of uneasiness on the part of any bird he approached, but this newcomer refused to defer. Instead, its vicious beak snapped repeatedly, as if cracking the hardest nuts, and its feathers fluffed to twice their bulk.

"Kr-rark!" he croaked angrily, sidling a bit closer, and a wheeling herring gull, about to investigate the whale, swerved off at the sound. But the stranger stood fast. Its wicked head pivoted until the wide eyes with their feline pupils glared insolently at the raven.

Maddened beyond endurance by such uncompromising treatment, Rark flung himself upon the intruder. There ensued a wild flurry of black and white. Catlike, the huge owl threw itself upon its back to bring the terrible claws into play, while Rark's powerful beak, guided by the hard-bought wisdom of a quarter-century struggle for existence, drove for a big yellow eye.

But somehow the eye shifted; the sharp bill stabbed by, while tufts of Rark's hard black feathers fluttered in the air as the owl's mighty beak ravaged the raven's breast.

The whole skirmish lasted perhaps twenty seconds, and it was Rark who withdrew, bedraggled and amazed, a feeling of profound respect in his arrogant heart. This was no buzzard! Only years of battle experience had saved the raven from serious injury even in that brief encounter. Frustrated, he paused some feet away to preen his torn plumage and take stock of the situation.

Presently, however, as he remembered the succulent blubber lying in vast quantities beneath his feet, his mercurial spirits rose, and he pecked voraciously at the tasty stuff.

While eating, he took care, purely as a routine precaution, to keep a watchful eye on the owl, noting with wonder that the stranger showed no interest in whale blubber. So engrossed did Rark finally become in his puzzled survey of the white bird that before he realized the danger, one of his feet was badly tangled in a tight loop of rubbery flesh.

When this frightening fact dawned upon him, Rark, although unusually intelligent even for a raven, went completely mad. With wildly beating wings he senselessly fought the terrifying restraint until he sank exhausted in a black heap, unable even to refurl his pinions.

By then the sun was setting, and a sound reached his ears that terrified him more than a shotgun at ten yards. It was a reedy squealing, unutterably evil and abandoned. There was only one type of beach prowler guilty of such abominable keening.

In the faint light he could just make out the leaping figures, lithe and furtive, with red eyes agleam. He heard the unique sound of long, bare tails trailing in the sand, and even his stout heart quailed. They were wharf rats!

Despite his awful position, Rark wondered why the white owl didn't take flight before the swift and murderous rats were upon it. Apparently the strange bird didn't understand the nature of *these* rats: huge, battle-scarred veterans, many over a foot in length from nose to tail.

But Rark, wise as he was, underestimated the capabilities of an arctic owl. In the frozen wasteland it called home, there was nothing else on wings that could challenge it in the air; and on the ground not even the smaller blue foxes were safe from its mighty talons. Comparatively light in weight because of its superbly designed flight structure of hollow bones and air-sacs, the owl was more than a match for many creatures double its poundage. It had taken iron frost and polar gale in its stride since leaving the egg ten years before. Only to the huge polar bears did the owl defer; aside from them it feared nothing, never having heard a gunshot.

As the piercing eyes fell upon the prowling rats, they glowed with deeper fire, and for the second time that day a pale shadow drifted soundlessly into flight. A monstrous rat, standing eagerly on its hind paws, sniffing the telltale air and squealing with unbridled bloodlust, caught one glimpse of an ominous mass against the sky. But before the alarmed rodent could drop to all four feet, cruel talons stabbed it through as the owl snatched its victim effortlessly aloft.

The marks of many a deadly battle testified to the fighting heart of the big wharf rat, and its long yellow teeth tore ferociously at the feathery thighs. Squeaking with pain and fury, it writhed and bit until the dispassionate owl, badgered into retaliation, achieved a miracle of aerial technique by driving its heavy beak deep into the rat's brain while still in flight.

The doomed creature's last cries rang over a deserted beach, for the army of rats had vanished. They knew, if Rark did not, how death was quartering the sands; and that for this night, at least, something sailed the air that no rat could face.

But the scent of the dead whale was irresistible, and before long a lean giant, one-eyed and gashed with countless scars, braved the moonlit beach. To Rark's horror this killer headed straight for him, its keen nose leading it directly to the living flesh it preferred. Atop the whale it paused briefly to survey with its one beady, satanic eye the trapped bird crouching there in silent desperation.

Twice the rat lunged in for the kill, only to be driven back, badly torn by Rark's powerful beak. Finally, shrilling with pain and rage, the rat cried for aid, a summons rats seldom disregard. Then, battle-wise in its way, with blood running from a deep slash perilously near its remaining eye, the rat feinted and leaped to Rark's back.

Before the raven could twirl on his trapped foot, the rodent's sharp incisors closed on the back of his neck. For one moment of blackest despair the fangs worked their way through the feathery armor to the life blood racing beneath, and Rark's choked cries blended with the mad flutter of his wings.

Then the puff of white floated ghostlike overhead, and for the first time there boomed over the quiet beach the appalling hoot of a snowy owl.

"Who-o-o! Who-o-o-m!" rang the mighty cry, and panic-stricken, the rat whirled to flee.

But the great yellow eyes, to which the pale light was as brightest day, followed unerringly, and flaming talons bit into the rat's vitals. As the agonized victim snapped frenziedly at the impervious thighs, the giant owl clenched its claws as a man might squeeze a sponge. In a single grating squeak of pain the life was crushed from the raging rat and its limp body carried off.

For a moment Rark cowered where he was, dazed and hopeless. Perhaps the random thought entered his mind that the owl would soon return to finish the job started by the rat. Yet, for the moment at least, the intervention had saved him. Then Rark became aware of a more important fact. In spinning to meet the attack, he had unwittingly freed the trapped foot to such an extent that a single determined peck could finish the good work.

It was time, too, for with its second catch the arctic owl, thoroughly rested, was flying back out to sea in search of the barren sub-zero world it loved; and the rats were again on the prowl. Rark launched himself wearily into the air just as one of the bolder rats pattered towards him.

And as the raven flapped his way to a certain snug perch, he turned his head to where a white form drifted seaward, and uttered a single soft "Ar-r-k!" It may have held a note of thanks.

The Fiery Patriot

When Colonel Hacker first saw the man some brass thought might be his savior, he gulped and did a double-take. This skinny buck private, with no chin—unless it had changed to an Adam's apple, since that was king-size—this kid, was he the one to pull a large rabbit out of a rather small hat?

But Hacker was a fair-minded officer, and took another look. He saw the steady, pale blue eyes, and thought briefly that Billy the Kid had performed a bit beyond his size, too. Besides, this boy, Private Selby, had been wounded at Guadalcanal as a volunteer member of a patrol. Anybody with the moxie to offer himself into a deal like that— Japs, jungle, the works—had distinct possibilities. Not that the colonel wanted guts as much as brains.

As for Selby—snatched out of his platoon and flown a million miles, give or take a few, to Washington, and now in this hotel room with a cold-eyed chicken colonel—he was a picture of bewilderment.

"Private Selby," the officer said, glancing needlessly at the folder, already memorized, in his hand, "I understand you once headed up an outfit called 'Ingenuity, Incorporated.' In Queens, before the war."

"Yes, sir," Private Selby said. "I was just getting started."

"It's just by chance—or luck—that we got a line on you," Hacker said. "A Major Temple happened to mention something about your getting a bolt out of the bottom of a narrow shaft when all the engineers were stumped. You weren't even part of the job. Only a kid looking on, I believe."

Selby seemed embarrassed. "Well, sir," he said. "It was just a sudden idea. I get them now and then. I've read a lot—science, mainly. I hoped to get to college, but my family didn't have money. After I'd come up with a few ideas for construction people—I knew a lot of them; always watching—I had this plan for a little company to solve tricky engineering problems. I was only beginning, sort of, when the Japs hit Pearl Harbor, so ..." His low voice just petered out.

"So you volunteered," Hacker said, with no particular expression in his voice. "Just how the hell did you get that bolt out, anyhow?" he demanded.

"They couldn't use a magnet," Selby said. "The bolt wasn't iron or steel. Because of a zig, they couldn't drop a sticky weight on a wire, either. My idea was to pour mercury, down, and let the bolt float up—which it did, being lighter, naturally, than the mercury."

The colonel coughed. "I see," he said. For a moment, he was silent, then he took a fresh tack. "We have a problem—a mighty tricky one. Not here, but in Occupied France," he added meaningfully.

The pale blue eyes flickered briefly. "Parachute?"

"I can't go into details until I know you're committed to the job," Hacker told him. "I can say this: it's dangerous. You'll be risking your life every minute, and the dying could be slow and painful. They use torture on agents."

"I've never jumped," the boy said slowly. He didn't add that he was afraid of heights. There were plenty of scary things on Guadalcanal, too, most of them being short, dedicated to the Emperor and quick on the trigger. What must be faced, you faced. There are worse ways to define a man.

"You can be taught," was the cryptic reply. "It's only one jump, not a career with the Paratroops. We have plenty of athletes. What we need is somebody with a wild imagination. At that, we're not hopeful. I'm told the job is really tough—not physically tough, but difficult, like a math problem, say."

The boy's eyes were glittering shallowly. He so loved puzzles, the colonel inferred, with some wonder, that he was willing to drop into enemy country, at the risk of torture and death, to tackle one. Well, it took all kinds, and maybe this was the kind they needed so badly right now.

"Interested?" Hacker asked drily.

"I'm ready," Selby said. "I'll do my best, but I'm not a professional engineer or scientist, you understand, sir. No degree. Nothing like that."

"I've talked to a mess of people with all kinds of degrees," Hacker told him. "If we could build a lab next to the spot, maybe their plans would work. But the Germans might not give us a building permit," he added, smiling tightly. Then he looked at his watch. "I'll lay it on the line. Time's getting short. There's a place in Occupied France— formerly a church—which has been taken over by a branch of German Intelligence. There are records in the loft that will soon be turned over to the Gestapo. Now, Army Intelligence is one thing. But if Himmler's boys get those dossiers, it means a slaughter, including quite a few innocents, and some friends we can't spare."

"What about bombs?"

"No good. The town's a thicket of flak towers, and a million top fighters—Focke-Wolfes—are stationed nearby. And what's worse, we can't get a man into the church at all. Security is absolutely one hundred per cent. How you can help, I don't know, but we're desperate."

"I don't speak French," Selby admitted cheerfully. "A few words of Italian and Yiddish are my limit. Except for '*Erin go bragh*'— which is useful, too, in New York."

"You won't have to. If you're seen, or questioned, you'll be a deaf-mute. One of our men will be with you, but French partisans are carrying the ball. They'll lead you to a spot near the church, and let your ingenuity take over. What we need, actually, is a fire. It's not possible, as I see it, ever to get enough explosives near the files to do the job. And blowing up papers doesn't always destroy them, anyhow."

"Fire?" Selby murmured. "From *outside* the church? How far away?"

"I should think a couple of hundred yards," the colonel said grimly.

"What do I work with?"

"Anything we have. A whole arsenal of incendiaries—big, little, tricky, simple. Plenty to choose from." He reached into his brief case and took out something the size of a cigarette. "If you could get one of these into the loft where the records are, that would do it, I think."

"Stone church?" Selby asked, a hint of anxiety in his voice.

"No. We don't ask the impossible. The loft is wood. There's probably a good deal of concrete or masonry in the lower parts, but that shouldn't matter. A fire down there would be stopped before it got very far, in any case. But up in the loft, on a Sunday night, say, when things are a bit slow, and most of the guards are outside ... You see my point." He gave the boy a long stare.

Private Selby shrank a little in his faded uniform.

"I'll have to see the place," he said. "That's the only way I ever get ideas."

"Fair enough. You'll leave for England tomorrow morning by plane, and should be in France a day or two later, depending on the weather and our contacts with the Underground. Any questions?"

"Where do I sign up for parachute lessons?" Selby asked, forcing a smile.

"They'll brief you in England. It's not much of a course. They'll probably just tell you to sag at the knees and roll when you hit. At least, that's all they ever told me. It's something that can't be practiced without a lot of fancy equipment—towers and stuff. Like Benning. One try, no repeats. But you'll make it," he added. "Others have." He pressed a button on the flimsy desk, and a big sergeant, immaculate in his MP uniform, came in. "Take him away, Larry," the colonel ordered. "He's all yours."

Three days later, Private Selby, to his own continuing astonishment, found himself rapidly approaching French soil, which was straight down. He had already relearned something taught him once at Guadalcanal: that a greater anxiety completely swallows a lesser. Filled with the excitement of landing in enemy country, and the risks to follow, along with his nagging fear of failure—after all, Ingenuity Incorporated had existed only briefly, and had solved few problems—the boy made the jump like a robot, his mind on more pressing matters.

There had been a moment of primitive terror at the free fall, followed by amazement at the unexpectedly strong jolt of the opening silk. But then had come the easy, actually pleasant, downward glide. His landing was made easier, too, by his low weight, and the OSS man who jumped with him helped by carrying most of the heavier equipment.

The next night, he lay on his middle, two hundred yards from the church, and wondered how to unscrew the inscrutable. The lower two-thirds of the building was brightly illuminated by floodlamps; and the soldiers patrolled ceaselessly, not only the immediate grounds, but the whole area, which had been carefully cleared of brush and trees.

Behind the screen of undergrowth just outside the patrol boundaries, Selby consulted with the OSS officer, Major Kalergis.

After a long look through powerful night glasses, the boy said, "That belfry over the loft's open on all sides. That would be a good spot."

"It would," was the sour reply. "Only we can't get at that tower—or any other part of the church."

"I was thinking of some kind of catapult, to toss an incendiary up there."

"We have just the gadget," Kalergis said. "It's a crossbow, modern style. It's used, among other things, to flip fire pellets into ships from the docks at night."

"Well, then ..." Private Selby replied.

"First of all," the officer interrupted him, "even if it could carry one of these lightweight little cylinders that far and that high, it would make quite a rap. There's a sentry inside that belfry night and day. If it came in, he'd see or hear it. And if you're thinking about the roof, he'd hear it there, too. I know," he added coldly, "because we tried it at the start, and lost three good men when a patrol charged out here about ten seconds after the pellet thumped the roof. We had to weight it to get the range needed."

Selby was silent for a moment. Then he said, "How about when the bell is ringing? The sentry couldn't hear much then."

"What bell, you dreamer? They melted that down practically the same day they occupied the town. Imagine them passing up good gun metal!"

The boy gulped, a sour taste in his mouth. This was tough—maybe too tough. He studied the belfry again, and saw a vague shadow detach itself to go sailing off over nearby fields. He saw it outlined briefly against the moon. No mistaking that shape, and the ghost-quiet flight of down-edged feathers.

"Owl," he said listlessly.

"He'll have his work cut out," the major said. "The peasants have eaten just about every rabbit in the area, and are beginning on the mice. Didn't the Romans go for mice, in honey, or something? Not for me! I'll take barbecued ribs!"

"Mice," Selby said, his voice edged with excitement. "We need some mice!"

"What?"

"Tomorrow's Sunday—right?"

"All day. Did I hear you say ..."

"It's our best chance—the colonel said so," the boy interrupted him. "Maybe—just maybe—we can pull it off."

"What the hell are you muttering about?" Kalergis demanded. "Let me in on it, if you've got an idea."

"No time now. Let's get out of here. I'll explain on our way back to the hideout."

The next night, the two men again lay just beyond the patrol area. Selby had eight freshly killed mice in a paper sack. He had also brought some black thread. Now that he was here, the whole scheme began to seem wildly far-fetched and ridiculous. Instead of a medal, he might get a Section Eight out of this deal. And yet ... and yet ... time would tell.

After a good deal of messy crawling about, and being constantly shushed by the OSS man, who was scandalized at his clumsiness, Selby finally found what he was searching for: a big tree stump. He put one of the mice in the center of it, and with deft fingers adjusted a springy twig so that, when tugged by the thread from ten yards away, it scraped and rustled against the wood. Fastened to the little corpse was one of the cigarette-sized incendiaries. Small as it was, he had been assured by the major that if two or three got a good, silent start on the roof, they would be almost impossible to quench. They spread molten metal and chemicals in a devil's mixture that ran and hissed, and consumed anything that was even remotely inflammable.

Patiently, the two men waited until the moon rose and the shadow floated free of the church tower. For some time, the big owl quartered the more distant fields, and the officer swore viciously under his breath. But finally, it drifted their way, and Selby, the back of his hand pressed tightly to his lips, produced agonized squeakings that would excite any famished predator. The call had often worked on owling trips at night in New York State. Surely these French owls had the same keen hearing as their American brothers!

The big bird dipped in its flight, and Selby pulled at the thread. Led unerringly by its wonderful ears, the owl swooped to the stump, snatched the mouse and quickly flapped off.

They caught a glimpse of its grotesque monkey face, and the boy muttered: "Barn owl. I'll be damned. Didn't even know they had 'em here."

Eagerly, they saw it return to its favorite spot somewhere on top of, or perhaps under the eaves of the belfry. Very soon it came back hoping for more, which Selby was delighted to provide. The owl took all eight mice, and quickly, which made Kalergis wonder at its capacity.

"They're pretty small snacks," the boy told him. "And from what you say, food's hard to come by here, even for birds." He peeked at the luminous dial of his watch and smiled at the officer.

"Fifteen more minutes, if you set 'em properly—sir." It occurred to him that he'd been pretty lax on military courtesy even with Colonel Hacker. But there was something sort of informal and all business about these OSS people. Still, he felt a bit guilty not observing all of the proper amenities.

"Will the owl swallow those bombs, or what?" Kalergis asked.

"Hardly likely," Selby said, wondering if the officer was serious. "It will get rid of those along with a few other parts of the mouse. My guess is, it'll cut the thread just as soon as it settles up there on the belfry."

"We really should make tracks out of here," the major said a little wistfully. "But I gotta see this."

"I'm with you," the boy said. "Besides, shouldn't we check it out—make sure?"

"The French would let us know, all right," Kalergis said.

Eighteen minutes later, a pinpoint of fierce, bluish light appeared on the roof of the belfry, and moments after, several others blossomed near it. Two more flared futilely at the base of the building, having rolled, no doubt, from the eaves. They came in handy by distracting the guards, who were so busy with these obvious fires that they missed for a time the more vital ones overhead. Then came a great turmoil, but the mighty little incendiaries were not easily reached, the Germans having no wings. Before long, the tower was a pinnacle of flame. The two men exultantly shook hands, then bolted for their hideout.

Some weeks later, Selby rejoined his outfit, but sworn to silence, was unable to explain very much. If he tended occasionally to hum the melody of "I Don't Want to Set the World on Fire," nobody really got the message.

The Room

As founder, president, and sole employee of Ingenuity, Incorporated—
this in pre-Pearl Harbor days—Private David Selby felt that the United
States Army was too hidebound. Not even the best ideas from a lowly
enlisted man ever got past the first sergeant. Selby never had any
doubt that he could have shortened World War II by at least a year, if
he could have found a sympathetic listener of high rank, but that didn't
happen until the OSS pulled him off Guadalcanal one day to help them
burn a church in Occupied France—from several hundred yards away.
He was listened to on that occasion, and did the job; but his
suggestions for reorganizing the whole Army were coldly ignored by
the OSS colonel.

But he had made his mark as an inventive, offbeat and highly
original saboteur with that single operation, and when the OSS had
another tough assignment—quite as impossible, it would seem, as that
of the inaccessible church—Private Selby was snatched away again,
much to the relief of First Sergeant Balko, who didn't know whether to
tear up the boy's twenty-page brief on a new way to site in artillery,
pass the buck to the battery commander, whose neck purpled at the
sight of any such paper on his desk, or send the formula-studded
disquisition direct to Washington.

Selby himself was apprehensive, not sure whether he was to be taken off for summary execution, or—what was almost as bad—to be handed another "impossible" assignment.

It was some relief to the boy, finding himself with Colonel Hacker, the same OSS officer who had briefed him on the last job. As for the colonel, he again felt a moment of doubt on seeing the almost chinless, skinny buck private for the second time in a year. He wondered briefly if the first success had been only a lucky fluke; certainly, the kid was not an impressive figure, at best; he looked too young to shave, was built like a garden hose and seemed ready to faint at a harsh word.

But Selby's pale blue eyes had a surface sheen like polished stone, and he was said to be a damned good man on a tough patrol. And Hacker knew very well, from his own experience, that the big, beefy, loud types weren't always the bravest men in a bad spot.

"How's your ingenuity these days?" Hacker asked the boy in a dry voice, as Selby was ushered into the Washington hotel room by an MP sergeant.

The private's huge Adam's apple, which the officer couldn't help thinking of as his missing chin, hiding out, bobbed up and down violently before Selby spoke. But his voice was surprisingly deep and steady.

"I never know that," he said, as if guarding himself in advance, "until I'm right at the source of the trouble."

"So you explained last time," Hacker said. "Well, history repeats itself. The trouble's still in Occupied France. Of course," he added cheerfully, "you're now an experienced paratrooper."

Selby gulped. He'd made only one jump in his life, and had been too worried about other things to be scared. Now, he wasn't sure he liked the idea of another drop.

"What kind of a setup this time?" he wanted to know.

"Could turn out very much like the last. I'll tell you about it right now. Sit down over there, and relax. I want your full attention, so forget rank for a while.

"There's a Gestapo HQ in Occupied France—a good-sized building. We have a man who's worked his way into the inner circle of collaborators, and naturally, he's been very valuable to us. But, unfortunately, he has come under suspicion. The top Nazis are going to hold a kind of private inquisition in a few days, and if they decide our boy's guilty, he'll be liquidated, and messily. It's impossible to get him out; he's already being watched closely. However, it was suggested that if extensive and severe sabotage took place in that building—in a room he's never had access to—it would not only get him off the hook, but make the Gestapo suspect its own top men. Only the big shots are permitted to go in and out of that room, and the floor is guarded tightly. There are records in cabinets that are apparently super-secret. Our man certainly hasn't been able to get close to them."

"I take it," Selby said shrewdly, "that's where I come in."

"Right. We don't expect you to crash the room, though. We're hoping you can suggest some way to make it look as if the place was sabotaged from inside—which would have to mean somebody in a Gestapo uniform—a big somebody."

The boy didn't say anything, just whistled softly.

"It's not quite that bad," Hacker said. "This will be an optimum period, so to speak. French workmen are doing odd jobs on the building—washing windows, removing ivy and birds' nests, some painting, stuff like that. We can get you in with them; that's no problem. There will be a day, maybe two—but don't count on it—when you'll be allowed near the one window. Unfortunately," he added, "it's nailed shut and covered with heavy hardware cloth."

"That's peachy-keen," Selby said, his voice wooden.

"I needn't point out," the colonel said, "that you can't leave any trace on window or screen; there must be no evidence of any operation from outside. That's why I asked about your ingenuity." He gave the boy a speculative stare. "It's tough, mighty tough. Frankly, none of our men could see a way. But they tend to think according to their own special training and official gadgets. You have a freer mind—I hope."

"Remember, I don't speak any French."

"You won't have to. We've a spot ready as the deaf-mute cousin of a partisan. He's one of those, by the way, who helped destroy key records of the district before the Germans took over. They still don't know who's who, so you'll pass for what we say—for a while, anyhow. You'll have a day or two to look around and be ingenious before the work party tackles that window area." He paused, and there was a pregnant silence for some moments. "Well?"

"Well, what?" Selby replied, pale eyes shining. "I can't say anything until I see the problem close in."

"Then you're willing to go."

"Yes, sir."

"I have to remind you it could be dangerous—even fatal."

"Sure, I know. But the Japs in the Pacific aren't using squirt guns, either," the boy said, grinning weakly. "Besides, if I'm away a while, Sergeant Balko might just cool down."

"Eh?"

"Nothing, sir."

And so, for the second time in a year, Private Selby found himself in Occupied France, dressed in the weird and outlandish clothes of a native workman. He was now Etienne Duclaux, the deaf-mute and slow-witted cousin of old Père Benoit, who owned the tannery. Benoit complained bitterly of having another mouth to feed, with food so scarce—*nom d'un nom!*—and was relieved to have the boy given unskilled chores around the Gestapo Headquarters building.

It was vital for Selby to have a look at the critical window before actual work near it began. Even the most ingenious person can't hope to solve a problem blind. The partisan in charge of him, who spoke passable English, managed to arrange this. There would be a preliminary inspection to check the growth of ivy, and estimate how long it would take to remove it. The Gestapo had ordered that the job be done during the lunch hour; they wanted no curious Frenchman, however ignorant or unlettered, peering through that particular window while certain documents might be open on the desks.

In a way, that was good, Selby thought. One of the key difficulties had been removed. Nobody, surely, could expect him to sabotage the blasted room from the outside, with no trace, while Germans were busy inside. It had to be done, if it could be done at all, while the place was empty. And one preliminary examination, while not much, was far better than none.

When the ladder was in place, just after noon, he climbed up, sweating in the hot sun, right behind Jean Martine, the senior in charge of the project. As the old man tugged at the ivy, and made marks in a shabby notebook, Selby studied screen, window and room with a degree of concentration that would have amazed some of his high school teachers, who always thought him a hopelessly fuzzy-minded daydreamer—which he was, at times. Like Newton, Jefferson, and some other prophets.

The screen was strong, new and large-meshed, the openings being about an inch square. The window, as he had been warned, was fastened down with heavy nails, but was clean, no doubt to maximize the amount of daylight in the room.

To his dismay, there was nothing in the place close to the window; any sabotaging would not only have to take place through screen and closed window, but from a distance of several feet, as well—which was plain murder. Selby's heart sank like a sack of cement in mid-ocean. The job was impossible. This didn't call for ingenuity; it begged for a miracle, and one so wild no church would give it standing.

It was a pity, too. The room was vulnerable to a tempting degree. There was a wooden cabinet a few feet from the window, its oily, polished surface shining in the sun. It would burn beautifully if torched. So would that stack of maps—the upper one cautiously placed face down on top of the others—on a table. The cabinet, he'd been told, was full of dossiers; its loss would be a great annoyance to the Gestapo, besides tending to clear the suspect. Yes, a pity, but nothing could be done. Moodily, Selby climbed down.

The actual work would begin Monday, at noon. This was Saturday, and nothing would be done tomorrow. So there was one day for him to come up with something. One or a hundred, it was all the same.

On Sunday, alone, he wandered glumly about the town, aware that it would be wiser to keep out of sight. After all, the Germans weren't fools; one of them might decide to see if old Benoit's cousin was really so useless. Men were needed all over France and Germany as laborers, especially able-bodied ones. This fellow would be around only a few days, it was said—he was just visiting the Benoits—but some ambitious *feldwebel* might decide to earn a commendation by finding another worker for the Third Reich.

But if Selby walked, he kept to the back streets, where traffic was light, whipping his murky brain for an idea, although his intelligence, viewing the problem with chill logic, told him firmly there couldn't be a solution. It was like the immovable body and the irresistible force—impossible by definition. You couldn't get from the outside of a room to the inside and not go through something, thus leaving a trace. Basic topology. If only there was a real, practicable fourth dimension!

He thought of drilling a tiny hole in a corner of the pane, and then using a hypo to squirt some incendiary fluid through the puncture to the floor. But it was a silly notion, not worth developing. The Germans were very thorough; they would find the opening, no matter how minute, infer the rest, and make the French workers pay a high price for the attempted sabotage. Glass was devilish stuff; you simply couldn't pierce it and cover up the tracks. Too hard, too brittle, impossible to repair.

All right. What about boring into the stone wall of the building instead? Fine. A hole in that rough material might escape notice, but it had to come out in the room, and that was bad, since plaster was no better than glass. It would chip or crack, maybe even a chunk of the old, crumbly stuff would fall. So that was out, too. The whole thing seemed impossible.

He was passing a drab little house, when he saw something just visible over the low stone fence that brought him up short. It was shrouded in canvas, but had a shape that couldn't be hidden from a knowing eye, particularly in such a location. And it stirred Selby's memories, reminding him of his own boyish investigations.

He stood there for a moment, staring and wondering, guessing at specifications. At the moment, he had forgotten his big problem; this was merely a diversion. Without a thought, he vaulted the fence, finding himself in the small yard with its one ancient apple tree.

Then he realized, as something cold stirred in his vitals, that somebody else was there, too.

"Be tranquil, my friend," the man told him softly. "I know who you are."

Selby, taut and pale, studied the speaker. Then he relaxed with a sigh. The pallid boy, a cripple with one arm, had been at a meeting of the Underground, and could undoubtedly be trusted. He had the hot, intolerant eyes of a fanatic, but all his hatred was directed toward the Germans.

"That belonged to Marcel Leconte, the schoolmaster," the boy said. "The Gestapo took him away last week. So I doubt he'll ever use it again. I was about to dismantle it before some greedy Boche sees it—and pouf!" He waved an eloquent hand.

It is doubtful that Selby heard him through. Because suddenly, like a flashbulb in his brain, he had The Solution. It was right here in this tiny garden. It would work; it had to work. Just a matter of some details, now. And weather—that great unpredictable. If that wasn't right, not a prayer ...

Tersely, he explained his needs to the boy, and the two got busy.

At noon on Monday, Selby stood on the ladder, waiting for the exact moment. The window overlooked a back street, and he could count on being unobserved, at least as much as anybody can in this irrational world. There is always some danger of an unseen witness—the old woman at a window, with nothing to do but spy on her neighbors; the bright-eyed child in the weeds, himself invisible, who sees far too much, and may talk, knowing little of adult fears.

But few Frenchmen would willingly betray him, and Jean Martine did his best to watch all points of the compass while shielding the boy as much as possible with bulky equipment in motion. It would take an exceptionally keen observer to catch Selby at work behind that screen of clippers, brooms, baskets and waving poles.

Timing was vital, and very tricky, so the agent waited until almost one before putting his plan into operation. He wanted to be well clear when the damage was discovered. None of the big shots who used this office was likely to return before two, but the Germans had ordered the work completed earlier. It was essential, too, that the sabotage be found promptly. If it went too far, the evidence proving an inside job would be lacking. For example, if heat cracked the window, the Nazis would never doubt that the whole job had begun from outside, and everything would be lost.

Meanwhile, he and Martine removed ivy in great, tangled lengths; that bit well done would help to alibi them later.

Finally, at twelve fifty-six, finding himself unobserved from below, Selby took from under his shabby jacket a great, glowing disc—the beautiful object lens of the schoolmaster's telescope. Nothing else could have done the job, but this glowing circle of optically flawless glass had a focal length of ninety inches, which meant that, unlike any simple magnifier, it could bring sunlight to a white-hot pinpoint of energy from almost eight feet away.

It would take a very imaginative Nazi, Selby told himself, to think in terms of such a focal length. And imagination was not a gift of the species.

The cabinet was his first target. As he'd hoped, it was quite inflammable, and he soon had the front drawer smoldering. The sky, fortunately, was almost free of clouds, the sun bright and hot over his right shoulder.

The nearest guard, Selby knew, was not at the door, but by the stairs, down the hall, which was good. The fire would be well along— but not too far advanced—and himself gone, when they discovered it.

When the cabinet was burning briskly, he set the maps afire; that was easier. The desk, unhappily, was not in good focal range, even when he moved the lens up and back as far as possible. But the locker was open, and he managed to start some uniforms smoking. Best of all, there was a big jar of nitric acid on the top shelf—why, he couldn't guess, although Hacker might have told him about Gestapo tortures. By bringing the spot of concentrated sun heat to bear just at the liquid line, Selby broke the glass, sending the corrosive chemical all over clothes and floor. If that didn't look like sabotage—and from the inside—nothing ever would, he reflected happily.

He didn't press his luck, but left right after, the two men having done as much work on the ivy as unwilling and underfed Frenchman might be expected to do for their oppressors.

"In other circumstances, with luck," Hacker told Selby later, back in Washington, "they might've lost the whole damned building. But in this case, it's a good thing they spotted the smoke fairly soon. Much more important to have the Germans think it was an inside job than to scratch their HQ." He gave the private a quizzical stare, as if still wondering about him. "It was a stroke of genius. I hear the top German brass think there's a traitor right among them—just as we hoped. And our man has been cleared. We'll get him out of France before very long. The pitcher that goes to the well too often, you know."

"They don't suspect the truth then?" Selby asked anxiously. "The schoolmaster has a family."

"Hell, they haven't the foggiest idea that it was done from the outside. They went over that window and the walls, too, with everything but X-rays. Naturally, they questioned old Martine, hoping that maybe he saw something, but they didn't push hard—for them. They have sense enough to figure that whoever did the dirty work—and inside, mind you—wasn't idiotic; he wouldn't start a fire with two workers on the ladder watching him. And Jean had no reason to mention you, so your leaving didn't bother anybody."

"Speaking of leaving," Selby said, "have my orders been cut yet? My first sergeant—Balko—should be calm by now. As calm as he ever gets—say, down to a hurricane." He grinned. "That guy hates ingenuity. He loves the Army Way."

"You can forget him," Hacker said, smiling in turn. "Any man who enlists owls, and turns a nighttime instrument into a sunlight saboteur doesn't belong with the dogfaces. From now on, Selby—and it will be Lieutenant Selby pretty quick, I think—you'll be working for the OSS."

He thought for a minute that the Adam's apple would bounce right up through the kid's head, but it settled down fast.

"Yes, sir," Selby said. "That suits me."

Dressed to Kill

Lieutenant Selby, of the OSS, very recently a mere infantry private, owed the sudden jump in rank to his ingenuity as a problem solver. Now, having carried out two almost impossible acts of sabotage against the Germans in France, the boy was rewarded—as all good workmen deserve to be—with an even tougher job.

"We have a man inside the factory—an Alsatian," Colonel Hacker told him at the briefing. "He's willing to blow up the machine, for a price. But there's just no way to get enough explosives into the building. The security's very tight; everybody who goes in is searched. It would take from three to five pounds of potent stuff to do a real job. And if we don't do it right, they'll be back in business in a hurry."

Selby nodded. He was a skinny, chinless boy, with enough Adam's apple for three, but his pale blue eyes were steady and cold.

"We can't bomb the plant, either," Hacker said. "It's underground, with several feet of reinforced concrete on top. Bristling with flak, too."

"What are they making that's so important? One lousy factory."

"Special electronic components for a new torpedo," the colonel said. "The wolf packs are bad enough, but if they get this gimmick into full production, it'll be murder. The subs could stand off the flank of a convoy, well beyond detection range, and send homing fish right into the middle of it. They can't miss—go right to engine sounds. This is their only machine right now. But it's all ready to roll, unless we stop it. If we can, it will take a long time for them to set it up again. Every day helps. We're beginning to lick the subs."

"Well," Selby said, "the whole problem then comes down to smuggling in explosives, it seems to me. I'll need to know a lot more about how the factory operates."

"You will," was the terse reply. "I'm sending you to France again. I think," he added with a tight smile, "you'd better continue as a deaf-mute. But there's not much chance of getting inside. You'll probably have to work through the Alsatian, Muller."

"What's his job there?"

"He's a technician, and can fuss around the machine. If you can find a way to get a few pounds of TDX or something to him inside the plant, he'll use it effectively. But not, I should emphasize, if they can pin anything on him afterwards. So you must remember that angle, too. All clear?"

"Yes, sir," the boy said ruefully. "Clear as cyanide in water!"

Corporal Muller turned out to be more than merely a paid informer. He was a World War I retread, never anything but tolerant toward the Nazis, but loyal to Germany. When his only son, after being badly shot up in Russia, came home with nasty stories of inadequate cold-weather equipment, command incompetence and the unspeakable treatment by the SS troops of women and children, there was trouble. The boy was hurried back to the East, and died miserably there in the frozen abattoir before Stalingrad.

So the Alsatian was bitter, and didn't care how soon Germany lost the war if the top brass got theirs at the finish.

Muller, stocky and blond almost to the point of albinism, had other grievances. His rank of corporal was too low for a man of his scientific ability, and the boss, Herr Doktor Brinckmann, a fanatical Nazi, was overbearing—and overrated. Selby, working patiently through a French partisan, had a hard time getting the corporal to the point that mattered most: how to blow up the key machine.

"I'm not sure there is any way," the Alsatian told him rather coldly. His manner made it clear that he didn't think much of this

American agent. How could a skinny boy, a young *lump*, handle so difficult an assignment? He added, "We can bring very few things with us in the morning, and they keep everybody there until six or later. Even for lunch, we have to take our own from home. Nobody can leave at noon. Except those like Brinckmann, who are above suspicion."

"Then you use a lunch box," Selby said, his eyes shining.

"Yes, but the guards look through it carefully. And even if they forgot, how much explosive can you carry in it? We don't get a lot of food—not these days," he grumbled.

The boy questioned him in great detail about operations in the plant, but the answers weren't encouraging. There was a crew of more than three hundred—mainly women—working inside, but only twenty-six dealt with the vital machine. Brinckmann supervised these, with the help of men like Muller.

"I'll have to get a peek inside, at least," Selby said gloomily, when he was alone with the partisan. "Any chance?"

The Frenchman looked doubtful.

"Maybe once," he admitted. "But it would be very dangerous for you and for us. That *salopard*, Brinckmann, he pokes his nose all over. If he should suspect you …"

The boy looked grave, his mouth tight. Then he said, "I'll have to risk it. Otherwise I'm stymied. So how do I get in?"

"A few Frenchmen do cleaning work and odd jobs there. You could go with them—in place of Lesage, who's sickly, and often has to send a substitute. Usually it's old Crain, but for once, his deaf-mute nephew might pass. If there's nothing in your present cover to keep you from being related that way. If we have to add more papers to those the form-crazy Boche loves, the risk is greater." He shrugged.

It is axiomatic that if anything at all can go wrong with a complex operation, you may expect the worst. In military planning, that's true in spades.

When the nine French workers, too old or incapacitated for heavy labor, were at the gate, being processed by a pair of bored but conscientious guards, Selby saw—and his stomach clenched like a fist at the sight—the approach of a tenth, who shouldn't have been there, of all places: Lesage himself.

Immediately, one of the guards, a hard-faced sergeant missing one foot, sounded off. Selby couldn't catch the words, but the message was plain.

"What's he doing here?" the German snapped, pointing at Lesage. "My sheet shows him out sick—again. I know where a good boot would cure the old malingerer," he added brutally.

Lesage, hollow chested and probably consumptive, shrank from the sergeant's hot gaze. He was obviously scared; somebody had goofed, forgetting to warn him.

Luckily, Selby's contact, Masson, had quick wits. With many gestures, he began to explain the mix-up, pouring out a stream of words so fast that Lesage had time to catch the drift and keep his mouth shut.

"He *is* sick," Masson said, indignation in his voice. "But you complain so much about his absences, the poor old one is quite terrified, and came here even though he should be home in bed. Now that he's come," the partisan added shrewdly, "you must use him, I suppose."

The guard's reaction came as expected. "Don't say 'must' to me, you French swine. You have too big a mouth. My paper shows a substitute for today—a Paul Durand. Is he here?"

Selby was about to step forward, but caught himself in time. Sweat dampened his forehead, and he cursed himself silently for a fool. Again Masson took over, his own face oddly white. He had noted the boy's half-step, and was still scared. Now he hustled Selby to the front.

"Paul's a deaf-mute, Sergeant," he said, "and almost an idiot, but good enough for rough, simple work. He's old Crain's nephew, here on a short visit," he added.

"Go home, Lesage," the sergeant said. "And you'd better get well fast—and stay that way. Any more malingering, and you'll be sorry. We're too easy with you pigs. The rest of you line up for the search."

The Germans feared such things as abrasive dust and chemicals, Selby guessed. A worker was lucky to get in with his clothes intact, so thorough was the examination of each man.

Once inside, Selby's job was that of scrubbing out stubborn stains on a tiled floor, using a heavy, clumsy, thick-bristled brush like a museum piece from the twelfth century. As he bore down with it, he had a good chance to sneak glances at the vital machinery he hoped to wreck.

As he cast one longer stare over his left shoulder, a mighty hand gripped his right one, and he was lifted almost bodily.

He found himself facing a huge man who seemed like a caricature of the typical Prussian. Brinckmann had a great, round head like a cannon ball; his deep-set grey eyes glowed with the consciousness of raw power; if he had a neck, it was invisible from the front. In a voice that seemed to rock the entire room, he roared at Selby.

Immediately, Masson hurried up.

"The lad's a deaf-mute, Herr Doktor. He doesn't know you want to see his papers. I'll make it clear." And he took out his own, jabbing them with a stiff forefinger. Selby played up, producing a fat handful of paper.

"Deaf-mute, is he?" the giant rumbled. "And French, I suppose. To me," he said ominously, "he looks German. A deserter, maybe, hidden by you scum. If so, I'll shake it out of him in a hurry."

Masson went livid; the matter was getting out of his control, and if Selby broke ...

This time, Muller saved the day. He skillfully adjusted some part of a basic machine so that it began to squeal and buzz. On hearing the noise, Brinckmann hastily dropped his victim, whirled, very lightly for so bulky a man, and charged toward the origin of the disturbing racket. By the time he was through flaying Muller and testing components of the machine, Selby was out of sight in a different corner of the plant, and Brinckmann seemed to have forgotten him for the present.

But although the boy had quick eyes, and used them well, he came up, at closing time, with exactly nothing. He was physically exhausted, but his air of dejection came from inside. The situation was hopeless.

The only person who could bring explosives into the plant was Brinckmann himself, and he was a poor prospect for the agent.

So Selby shuffled along with his companions, conscious of his raw and smarting hands. He wondered what in hell to tell Hacker, who obviously expected results. Two miracles down weren't enough; now they wanted a third. In his present mood, the new lieutenant began to look back on an island full of fanatical Japs, leeches and malaria as a Paradise Lost.

At that moment of despair and self-contempt, his eyes rested blankly on the bent back and meager form of the man just ahead of him. Selby's gaze suddenly focused and became sharp. An idea was forming in his mind, and it, too, began to take a definite shape. But was it practicable? Would it really work? He didn't know enough chemistry to be sure. But the scheme certainly deserved to be checked out by an expert.

Selby no longer felt tired, and forgot the throbbing of his blistered hands. He could visualize an intriguing plan, if the basic notion was sound. The Germans wouldn't know for days how the damage was done. But could Muller come out clean? That might take some more thought.

Back at the OSS field headquarters in London, the new lieutenant had an uncomfortable few minutes with his superior. But Hacker cared less about being a hard-nosed GI than getting the job done.

"I just don't know," the boy said. "The idea's really wild, and I'd like to talk with a pro before telling you anything about it."

The colonel had a perfect right to the information, however vague, but knew that insisting on one's rights was not always wise. In some ways, this chinless kid with the offbeat mind baffled him. But Selby *did* produce, so why cross him just to pull rank?

"There's a full professor from Cal Tech available for our work," he said. Then he added dryly: "Will he do, or would you prefer a boffin from our British pals?"

"The Cal Tech man would be fine," Selby said, flushing.

"Take this to him—that's the address," Hacker said, scribbling a chit, and the boy scurried away, feeling queerly guilty. He was withholding information from a chicken colonel; but he would rather seem uncooperative than nuts. The idea was fantastically wild, after all.

In a Germany fighting the rest of the world, and plagued by shortages of all sorts, there were bound to be times when the most essential machines had to stop briefly for lack of raw materials. In the case of Brinckmann's pet, this happened five days after Selby's inspection, when the supply of tungsten ran out.

It was the moment Muller had waited for. The machine was stopped and untended; none of his fellow workers need be killed in the explosion to come.

There was no warning, just an ear-shattering roar, and the huge complex, brought to operating perfection only after months of exacting adjustment, became a pile of junk. Several men were injured by flying chunks of metal, but nobody was killed. There was no explanation for the disaster—at first. Some notion of the cause would develop after technical experts went over the scene with scrupulous care.

"Let me get this straight," Hacker said to Selby, again back in London. "You got a smock just like the ones they all wear. And Professor Lansing confirmed your idea that by soaking the material—cotton—in nitric and sulphuric acids, you could make it into nitrocellulose: guncotton."

He reflected, not for the first time, that it had been damned clever of him to capture this kid from the infantry. One rifleman less on Guadalcanal, and how much materiel, how many Allied lives saved from German torpedoes!

"What about a detonator?" he demanded. "Doesn't guncotton need a blasting cap or the like?"

"The top button of the smock," Selby said. "Made of softish alloy. When Muller squeezed it, a tiny vial of acid broke, and ate through a wire, releasing a spring-loaded firing pin. That hit a primer—and *zowie!* When I remembered how they all took off their smocks and draped them every place—even on or near the machines—well, that gave me the idea. One smock equals about four pounds of guncotton, enough to wreck anything."

"Damned ingenious, Lieutenant," the colonel said. Then he gave the boy a sharp stare. Selby was chuckling.

"You don't know the topper," he said. "Muller balked at first; he's technically trained himself, and no fool. He told me they'd be sure to figure out from the shreds of material what had happened, and he'd be remembered as leaving that night without his smock. Stick out a mile, too, with all the others wearing or carrying theirs. Then, curtains for the corporal!"

"But you evidently convinced him. How?"

"I knew he took about the same size as his boss. And Brinckmann's the only one with free entry to that floor. Now, if in the excitement, Muller put on the Herr Doktor's smock, and if, as usual, the boss left later, the guards would see who was short one kraut coverall."

"So by now," Hacker said, grinning hugely, "Brinckmann may be having an interview with the Gestapo."

"It couldn't happen to a nicer guy," Selby said, his eyes pure arctic ice.

Last Gasp

When Colonel Hacker of the OSS loaned Lieutenant Selby, his "ingenuity man," to a British bomb-disposal unit, he was careful to impose one vital condition. "I don't want the boy meddling with any live land mines at close range. It's not his business, for one thing; and besides, I need him. He gets the wildest ideas since Rube Goldberg, but so far, they've worked every time. So I don't want his head blown off. Just give him a good briefing on your problem, and he just may come up with an answer. It has been known to happen."

"I understand," Major Duncan said. "Can't blame you, sir." A faint twinkle appeared in his tired eyes. "I'll wager a pound—which isn't much to you Yanks, I know—that old Brenner's too foxy for him. As he's been for us, blast him!"

"You're on!" Hacker said. "Let's say thirty days. Okay?"

"Righto."

The colonel's condition was obviously reasonable, but it didn't endear Selby to Lieutenant Niven-Blake, one of the unit's four survivors.

"I don't see how he can help us much from two hundred yards away, behind a bunker," he said, giving Selby a somewhat contemptuous stare. "Mighty careful of their men, the bloody American Army!"

"Put a sock in it, Leftenant," Major Duncan said sharply. "It wasn't his idea. Colonel Hacker insisted on it—and he's right. Bomb disposal's our pigeon, not OSS's."

Niven-Blake scowled, but kept still. He was small, emaciated and obviously near the breaking point. Selby's eyes briefly became polar ice, and his huge Adam's apple bobbed. But he wasn't there to brawl, and he guessed that anybody who'd seen a dozen friends blown up by a trick delayed-action bomb, fitted with too many booby traps, had a right to be edgy.

The other two members of the unit, Sergeant-Major Shanks and Corporal Doyle, were also tense and tired but not hostile.

"Let me brief you," the major told Selby. "Most of the bombs have fallen on London. That's where a big, delayed-action parcel is the most trouble, and the Germans know it. We can't blow them up on the spot, you see, without destroying flats. And so far, nobody's been able to de-fuse one of the tricky beggars."

"What's so special about these—compared to the others, I mean?" Selby asked.

"I don't know how much they taught you about such devices," Duncan said, "but delayed-action bombs are booby-trapped so that nobody can disarm them without sweating blood. These pets of Brenner's ..."

"You mean you know who makes 'em?"

"Oh, yes. There's the lettering on every one so far."

"He signs 'em?" Selby gulped.

"More than that—there's a message. Always the same. 'To Cheviot and Company from Old Boy Brenner.'"

"Who's Cheviot and Company? And why the special hate?"

"It's not really important," the major told Selby, impatience in his voice. "Just an old grudge, I suppose. We know that Brenner went to school with old Cheviot—he's a general now; strictly a mapwallah. That was years ago—eighteen ninety-seven or the like, I fancy."

"But why does Brenner have it in for him? And what about that 'and Company' bit?" the American persisted.

"I've no idea," the major said brusquely. "All I know is that Brenner spent a few years at one of our public schools, Cantwell. A good many Europeans did that. Now he's a bigwig boffin in Germany, and playing these monkey tricks on us while addressing his bombs to Cheviot. As if any general ever gets blown up. Only we bloody idiots in bomb disposal—and the civvies in London."

"I see," Selby said. "But you were about to explain how these bombs were different. I know about vibrators—various elements that quiver at the slightest jar, and complete a circuit to set off the charge. And chemical units—say, a spring-loaded pin that breaks a vial of acid, starting a different explosion. But I suppose that's kindergarten stuff in your racket."

"That's an understatement," Duncan said. "Maybe I'd better tell you the story of Brenner's bomb just as it happened.

"Two men, Crofts and Harkness, dealt with the first one. The casing foxed them; it was the type we call Mark VI. Very common. Only that blasted lettering was different, but it didn't bother them. After all, our own chaps are always writing notes to Hitler and Goering the same way. So do yours, I'm told. So they thought it was just another piece of cake, since they'd safely disarmed dozens of the things before. This time, they no sooner removed the cover, than the bomb exploded. As they worked, they were talking over a telephone to one of our men a safe distance away, telling him about every little step. It didn't help in his case. All we know is, off came the cover, and up went the bloody bomb." His voice became more dry and bitter. "And two good chaps with it.

"So we got clever. The next man just loosened the six screws, cemented the end of a thin wire to the plate, and backed off several hundred feet. The moment he tugged at the line, the bomb exploded. We lost another acre of housing.

"Well, it was obvious that Brenner had put a booby trap under the cover plate, so one of our technical advisers suggested that we X-ray the nose and find out what the real problem was. That seemed reasonable, so we got a portable unit and had a go. The second our radiologist turned his contraption on, the bomb exploded, killing him. So far, we'd bungled three of Brenner's specials and lost as many men. Not to mention the flats and the evacuation. It was a bad show.

"But that put us on the right line for a bit. The boffins decided Brenner must have a light-sensitive element under the plate. Something that reacted to ordinary daytime brightness, but also X-ray and maybe even infra-red. Which meant either removing the cover in the dark, or cutting through some other part of the casing. Well, to cut the blasted story short, we couldn't do it. When we tried cold chisels, the vibration blew up the bomb right off. With a torch, it was the same. There are devices that react to the slightest movements or jarrings, and others that are highly heat-sensitive. Brenner hadn't missed a trick."

"Guy's a genius," Selby muttered.

"But you're a match for him," Niven-Blake said. "Or so your colonel tells us."

"Look ..." the American began, a steely edge to his voice, but Major Duncan waved him to silence.

"You're tired, Leftenant," he told Niven-Blake. "Go and turn in. You're excused." Niven-Blake got up, leaving wordlessly.

"He's really quite a decent chap," Duncan said apologetically when the officer had gone. "But he's almost around the bend. We all are, thanks to Dr. Brenner."

"I understand," Selby said.

"Well," the Scot said, "I'll try to move faster with the briefing. We used a faint, red light, just barely enough to work with. Waited until dark, naturally. Our man was then able finally to get through the cover plate and remove the photo cell he found there. But one more trap showed up. A kind of diaphragm—circular, about five inches across. It was covered with wire mesh, rather fine, and coarse cloth behind that. We haven't any idea what the thing hides or how it operates. It's tied in with at least one vibrator element, because the moment it's moved, the bomb goes up.

"But there's worse. The chap who removed the plate and photo cell put a regular flashlight on the diaphragm, and nothing happened. Then he took a closer look—that's all he did: just *look*—and the bomb exploded!"

"But that's impossible," Selby exclaimed. "Nothing's sensitive to a human glance."

"We know that—or thought we knew it. But the last two men died trying to disprove that sight could be a trigger. After licking vibrators, heat-sensitive traps, photo cells—and the routine devices, too. He adds those now and then, just for fun and games. After all that, we're beaten. We can't get past that diaphragm. That's why," he added, giving Selby a quizzical, faintly humorous stare, "I accepted Colonel Hacker's offer of you. Maybe your Yankee ingenuity can solve the puzzle."

For the first time, the sergeant-major spoke. "Is it true, sir," he asked the officer, "that you bet a pound with the colonel that the leftenant can't do it? Me and the corporal 'ere thought as 'ow the leftenant might like to lay a bet with us."

Selby reddened, but Major Duncan cut in quickly. "It was the colonel's idea. The leftenant hasn't promised a thing. It's not fair to expect that. I say to drop it, here and now. Is that clear?"

Judging from their chopfallen looks, Selby knew it was.

"I think, sir, you forgot to mention the motor," Doyle said.

"Ah," the major said, "so I did. It seems, Selby, that after the bomb arms itself, a motor starts up somewhere behind the diaphragm. We hear it in our microphones. Battery-operated, no doubt. What it does, I can't say."

Selby looked thoughtful. Then he said diffidently, "One thing that does occur to me now is that sound may be the angle. If the man talks near that diaphragm …"

"Damn!" Major Duncan said softly. "We shouldn't have missed that."

"I could be way off," the American said. "But it's easy to check. Next time, don't do any talking near the mesh. Have the man back off each time he reports."

"Worth trying," the major said, and Shanks nodded agreement.

"If the Herr Doctor is on schedule," Duncan said, "we should get a package on Thursday. Consistent swine, Brenner."

His prediction was verified. A bomb fell, and Selby was at the listening post at night with Major Duncan when Doyle tackled it. They waited tensely as he worked under a dim red light, getting down to the diaphragm.

"All right, sir," he said then, his voice thin and metallic over the phone. "I'll start on the four little screws that hold the mesh. Won't say a word until they're out."

Several moments of almost unbearable suspense followed. Then came the rocking, ear-shattering roar of the explosion which seemed to tear at their guts. Selby felt sick, and Duncan's voice was several degrees colder as he said, "It isn't talking, either. Brenner's still ahead of the game." Then, more softly, "Poor old Doyle. A good man."

At the conference the next morning, where a new volunteer, Ferris, was introduced, Selby found the atmosphere rather chilly. But he ignored it, and said, "Sir, I'd like permission to talk to General Cheviot."

"What on earth for?" Major Duncan asked. "He doesn't know anything about this business."

"But he knows about Brenner: what the man's like, and why the personal hate. It could help. It might give us a clue about that diaphragm."

"Well," the Scot said, "there's no other bomb to deal with now, so I won't object, although it's a waste of time. I warn you—the general's a prickly old bargee. But he may be on his best behavior for an American—I don't think!"

When Selby got to Cheviot later that day, he found a short, brisk man, with a huge, indomitable Wellington beak above a typical guards' mustache. His eyes were a cold grey, yet oddly enough, he had a warm smile and spoke softly.

"So you want to know about Brenner," he said. "Hah! It was a long time ago, but I remember him—and obviously he still remembers Cheviot and Company. Stalk stuff, dontchaknow. Kipling was big then, and we—my friends and I in the Fifth Form—copied him. Well, sir, Brenner was a sneak and a coward. Water funk. A bully, too, when he could find some inky little fag to knock about." He broke off.

Selby had to prod him. "Please try to remember, sir; it may be important. What did he have against you, in particular?"

"Wish I knew," the general muttered darkly. "Those messages on his bombs are damned annoying. But I really had nothing to do with the brute. He was never my fag. Messy beast, he was. I know that. Didn't like to wash in cold water—all we had back then. Once we even had to use a wire brush on him, and a scrub-brush on his teeth; he never cleaned them. Funked the dentist, too; breath like a polecat. So Cheviot and Company took him in hand. A bit cruel, but that's how things were in ninety-eight. Because of his dirt and messin' about with chemistry, we called him 'Stinks'—'Stinks, the Prooshian!'"

There was little else he could tell Selby, but the boy wore a thoughtful expression when he left. An idea had already taken form in his mind.

At the next briefing, he laid his fantastic theory on the line.

"It has to be breath," he said, with more conviction than he felt, considering the extreme ingenuity of Brenner, a quality the OSS man was particularly able to appreciate. "Warm, moist air from the mouth. Obviously, the guy working on the diaphragm has to get his face close to those little screws, especially in a lousy light. And the motor, I think, must operate a sort of blower in reverse. Suction, pulling the breath down a pipe or something to where it can activate a detonator."

"And how does it do that?" the major asked coldly.

"I don't really know," Selby admitted, "but there could be ways that the warmth and humidity could trigger a device."

"And I'm to risk another man on that?"

"No," was Selby's quick reply. "I've been thinking that we could very easily rig up our own blower—a hair dryer, perhaps—and check out the next bomb by remote control. If warm, damp air actually sets it off, then we'll know how to handle it. Some kind of a face mask, probably."

"You're daft," Shanks said. "Breath setting off a blooming bomb!"

"Remember," Selby said patiently, "that Brenner was given a bad time over his personal hygiene—mainly bad breath. He never forgot it, and now he tries to get back in a weird, but workable way. That's why there's a message to General Cheviot and his old gang. I know it sounds crazy, but everything fits pretty well."

"All right," Major Duncan said. "We don't have much to lose with a remote control arrangement. I just hope the next one isn't near a populated area, so we can blow it up without getting wigged by HQ."

The wish came true. A Brenner bomb fell in a ploughed field, and Selby's scheme was put to the test. A battered electric hair dryer, supplied with moist cotton batting at the mouth, was set up to blow air against the diaphragm, once the booby trap was exposed.

But when Duncan closed the switch, nothing happened. They waited ten minutes, saturating the mesh with damp, hot air, but no explosion followed.

"Brenner wins again," Niven-Blake chortled, forgetting in his malice that a victory for Brenner meant trouble for the unit.

"I don't get it," Selby muttered. "I could have sworn ..." Then he slapped his head. "What a dope I've been!"

"Hear! Hear!" This from Niven-Blake.

"Another idea, Leftenant?" the major asked sardonically, looking at Selby.

"The same one—repaired, sir. You see, breath isn't just warm, moist air. We should have known that wouldn't do. Hell, with sun on the casing, and humidity, the bomb might go off any time. No, what was missing is the high concentration of carbon dioxide in human breath. Remember, Brenner's a chemist first. It would work," he added, half to himself, "with a photo cell and a glass case full of limewater. When breath hits that, it gets milky, and blocks some of the light. Then, blooie! All we need to lick it is a face mask, or even a pad soaked in limewater."

Duncan said, "Care to try it, Harry?"

Niven-Blake was pale. For a moment, he didn't answer. Then he snapped, "What's the odds? I think the Yank's crackers, but there's the same job to do. My turn, isn't it, so why all the palaver?"

A hasty trip to the nearest chemist's shop produced limewater, from which a mask was made. The usual phone line was set up, and Niven-Blake went to his lonely, dangerous post. The others didn't notice in the dark that Selby also slipped away. But Niven-Blake, his heart thumping as he reached out toward the tricky diaphragm, found the OSS man at his side.

"What the hell you doing here?" he blazed. "Mizzle off, you bloody young fool. It's not your pigeon. You want to get blown to rags?"

"You heard about that bet," Selby said, his blue eyes cold. "And there was another one Shanks and Doyle wanted to make. Well, this is all my doing—my idea—and I'm gonna bet, too. I bet my life I'm right this time. You touch that phone," he added in a hard voice, "and I'll flatten you and unscrew the mesh myself. And I'm pretty clumsy at times, I warn you."

Niven-Blake's teeth flashed in a tight grin, highlighted by the standing lantern.

"Have it your own way, you fool Yank," he said. "But before I touch the diaphragm, let me apologize. I was wrong about you, Selby. Anyhow, I'm betting my life again, even if it wasn't intentional!"

With a pad of cotton, well soaked in limewater, over mouth and nose, he adjusted the screwdriver and began, ever so gently, to loosen the mesh.

Selby's heart was pounding unbearably, much to his surprise. He had never before known this kind of tension, even in tight spots. The vision of a sudden explosion, a fiery cataclysm that might tear him to little bits, made his legs tremble. He felt an almost irresistible urge to run.

"Knock it off!" he told himself. "You won't even know it's happened—if it does."

As the first screw came out, Niven-Blake sighed softly, a mere ghost of a sound. The other three screws seemed anti-climactic. Then he pulled the mesh free, in slow motion and smoothly. Selby stared, unblinking, his jaw muscles so tight they ached. Would the bomb blow now? What if his idea was all wrong?

Behind the diaphragm was a metal tube, and in it a glass vial full of clear liquid. The American's heart leaped at the sight. Surely that must be limewater. And he guessed there was a photo cell beyond it.

"Light source," Niven-Blake said, pointing to a lens just opposite. "You could be right, Selby."

The OSS man pulled a bit of fluff from a pocket and held it near the mouth of the tube. It was sucked from his fingers.

"Q.E.D.," he said. "The thing sucks air—and your breath—in. Whaddya know! All miniaturized, too. Quite a job."

"Don't rejoice too soon," Niven-Blake said sourly. "Many a slip—and Brenner's a downy bird. May be another surprise."

Selby gulped. He realized you didn't ever relax at this work—not until the detonating charge, or charges, were several feet away from the bomb. Right now, after "solving" the puzzle he could still be atomized. *Be right, but dead right.*

With deft hands, Niven-Blake used a needle-nosed wire cutter to sever the copper lead. Now this ounce of limewater would start no current, milky or not. The Brenner bomb was harmless.

At OSS HQ in London, Selby reported to his superior, omitting his own disobedience of orders in standing by at the disarming.

At the end, he said, grinning, "That was a mighty ingenious gimmick for a detonator. I figure we ought to call Brenner's invention 'the last gasp of a desperate foe.'"

Hacker's iron face softened; his lips twitched, and he snapped, "Get out of here. You need a twenty-four hour pass. Last gasp! Don't we wish it!"

Murder of a Priest

After the horrors of Guadalcanal, where green American troops, wanting strongly to live, met Japanese veterans anxious to die for the Emperor, Lieutenant Selby considered himself shockproof. So far, his stint with the OSS had not disillusioned him. But now he stared at Colonel Hacker, gulped, and stammered, "Kill him? Me? You mean you want me to kill a—a priest!"

Colonel Hacker's face was set like iron; his eyes were somber.

"It's a dirty war," he said. "And this is a dirty job. But absolutely necessary."

Selby hesitated for a moment, thinking in a vague way about the phrase "Direct disobedience of orders." You don't just say "No" to a colonel.

"I can't," he said finally. "It's not for me. Anything else, okay. But to murder an innocent man—a priest!"

Hacker's eyes narrowed, and for a moment they looked as alarming as the muzzles of two pistols. But when he spoke his voice was level, almost toneless.

"Before we start going around in circles," he said, "you'd better have the whole picture. It may knock out some of that righteousness." Selby flushed darkly, but the colonel went on as if he had seen nothing. "Our contact in the French Resistance is yelling for quick help; their whole organization is in danger of being smashed—"

"But damn it, sir—one man isn't supposed to know that much! I thought they had tight little cells, with each one completely independent from the others, with nobody wise to men in a different group."

"That's true, in general," Hacker said. "But this once things got out of hand. The priest not only was active in his own cell, but he heard things at confession. It was risky, but seemed necessary at the time. Anyhow, his cover was very good, and except for bad luck they'd have gotten away with it. But Father Placide was rounded up with a bunch of hostages—the Germans want the name of the man who shot General Lindorf, so as usual they're holding women, children, priests—anybody handy.

"Hell of it is, somebody or something got them suspicious about Father Placide. They have some they think are bigger fish—the Gestapo means to work them over first. But in a few days at the most they'll get to Father Placide, and he'll break. He's over sixty, dedicated—all the guts in the world—but he'll talk. They all do. The Resistance knows it; we know it. Just a matter of time. Nobody can hold out indefinitely when the Gestapo really bears down hard."

"He could kill himself," Selby said, making his voice harder than normal. "Isn't that the usual way out? I mean—he doesn't *want* to help the Germans. And you say he's a brave man."

"Sure," the colonel said dryly. "I guess you're not a Catholic, Lieutenant. Father Placide couldn't possibly take his own life—that's a mortal sin. That's why—" Hacker gave Selby a cold stare—"he's passed the word to his friends that they're to do the job for him. I'd call that pretty brave, wouldn't you?"

Selby reddened again.

"You win—I guess. But it's still a dirty job, and I don't see where I come in at all. Some other Frenchman in the bunch with him—right on the spot—could do it. You don't need any special talent to kill an old man who isn't even going to fight back. Damn it, Colonel—"

"It's not that simple," Hacker said, surprisingly patient. He didn't say so, but he would have taken a queasy dislike to anyone who had accepted this assignment cheerfully. Selby's reaction to the job was that of any decent man even in a dirty war. To kill the enemy in the field, with both of you armed and menacing—that was one thing; assassination of an old man—that was another.

"They're holding Father Placide in one room, alone. As I said, they've been tipped he may know something. Now nobody from the outside can get to him—that's the problem in a nutshell."

"What's the building like?" Selby asked.

"It used to be a seminary of some kind. Lots of rooms not much different from prison cells except for such rudimentary comforts as running water—cold—johns, and central heat. I doubt if the present occupants get much use out of any of those.

"It's a big solid building in the heart of town, and as Gestapo HQ it's damn well guarded. Father Placide's cell is one of those without a window; I guess they have—or had—lights of some kind, maybe even electricity. But there he is, tucked away in the middle of the place, behind a heavy door, and due to be questioned any day now. And it's either him or dozens of key men. That's the story."

"Why the hell don't the others—the ones in danger—run right now? Wouldn't that be much simpler?"

"No," Hacker said brusquely. "They're not isolated individuals. They have families, relatives, friends. If the actual fighters and saboteurs clear out, they might make it alone to England or Spain. But the organization would be ruined for months, maybe forever. There aren't so many men who can do the jobs at the top, believe me. And besides, they'd have to leave wives and children behind. The Germans would grab them immediately, either for revenge, or to force the leaders back—the same old hostage bit.

"No, Lieutenant, it has to be Father Placide. It's what he wants, and it's what the situation calls for. Sure, it's a dirty job, but keep telling yourself about the alternatives."

Once more the colonel's eyes bored into Selby's. "You'll be leaving tonight. No plane this time. Small boat across the channel—it's a coastal town."

"And I'm supposed to kill a man inside a windowless room in Gestapo HQ," Selby said, almost to himself. "Nothing to it." His huge Adam's apple bobbed. "I'll use voodoo—damned if I can think of any other way."

"You will," Hacker assured him with a tight, mirthless grin. "You're an expert at puzzles—especially impossible ones."

Selby's trip was uneventful except for seasickness, a specialty of those choppy waters. That kept him from making even the vaguest or wildest plans—which was just as well, since anything conceived of before studying the building was not likely to work.

In his by now familiar role of a retarded Frenchman—a nephew of old Dr. Morin—he was able to walk the streets, but very cautiously, as the Germans, their hands full of hostages, and the town a powder keg, were edgy.

His first examination of the former seminary didn't help his confidence, already far from high. Deep inside he heard a nagging voice that whispered slyly: *Try and fail! It's too tough—you can't do it, anyhow. So fail, and let the priest's blood be on somebody else's hands.*

It was advice hard to ignore. The job might very well be literally impossible. Why fight it, then? Who can unscrew the inscrutable?—as the old word-play went.

But then he'd recall Colonel Hacker's comment. The alternatives—the equally impossible alternatives! Maybe twenty good men would be captured, tormented, slaughtered. Or if they ran, their families would suffer—indescribably. One life against many—that timeless, searing, heartbreaking moral dilemma, so often debated in theory, so terrifying in stark fact.

Reluctantly Selby made his choice. If there was a way to kill Father Placide he would have to find it. Maybe, with luck, he could then pass the ultimate move on to others ...

But the big building, a mass of grey stone, with only two doors, both guarded constantly, seemed invulnerable. Even if the Resistance made a suicidal foray, attacking frontally, they could never reach Father Placide's cell. It was on the second floor, accessible only by a long corridor. There were more soldiers up there, in a guard room. And a hundred yards from the building a battalion of the Wehrmacht had its barracks. Sure, they were older men, retreads, but their machine-pistols were new, their armored cars formidable.

"Isn't there anybody inside the place to help us?" Selby asked, peering at the gloomy faces in the kitchen of Morin's house. "Not a single man of yours there?"

"Yes," Roget told him sourly. "We have two. But they cannot get near the actual cells; they are kept on the first floor."

Roget was a dark, blocky, hairy man, even stronger than he looked. His English was excellent, and he acted as the American's interpreter.

"We can get messages to Père Placide—sometimes; but that is all. No gun, no poison—even if he would use them; but he will not." Himself a freethinker, Roget spat. "Afraid of a mortal sin! Me, I'd be afraid of the Gestapo—and of betraying my comrades."

The others glared at him.

"Père Placide is a saint," Dubois snapped. "Be quiet, you filth!"

"This is bad," Selby cut in quickly, fearing a brawl. He needn't have worried. They were all in the same war—Catholic, Protestant, Atheist, Communist, Anarchist; right now there was only the common enemy. Afterward, of course …

"No ideas, M'sieur?" Dr. Morin asked him.

"Not so far," Selby admitted, his face glum.

One of the younger men, shrugging, pulled out a sheet of paper, and by the dim light of an ancient oil lamp he began scribbling. This behavior, in the circumstances, seemed so odd that Selby craned his neck to look.

What he saw was something quite unexpected, something that took him back several years, to before the war. Surely this French boy couldn't be trying—but he was; no doubt about that. Three rectangles above, three below, and he was drawing lines.

"I'll be damned!" the lieutenant breathed, and the boy, seeing who was watching, flushed.

"*Quoi?*" he mumbled.

"Tell him it can't be done," Selby said to Roget. "You can't connect the upper and lower rectangles with three lines each—not without crossing a line. They usually state the puzzle as three houses with—"

He broke off, ignoring a constellation of gaping stares. "By God!" he added in a low voice.

"What is it, Lieutenant?" Roget asked. "You have thought of some way, *hein?*"

"I don't know—maybe. Can you get me a plan of the building?"

"There would be blueprints at the Mairie. But we know already about all the rooms, and the corridors, the roof, the basement—"

"No," Selby said sharply. "Not those." He looked slowly around the room at each man in turn. "I just remembered that even the most closely guarded house always has three open roads. The Germans won't be watching those."

He knuckled weary eyes. "I have to figure this out. What do we need? A hand drill, a big syringe—the kind a horse doctor might have. Hmm. Is there a photographer in town? Or an etcher? Say, a drug store—no, I mean—do you call him a pharmacist or chemist, like the English?"

Aware that his voice had a touch of hysteria, he regained control. Then slowly, in a low, calm voice, he explained how to murder Father Placide, patriot, priest, and martyr …

Back at OSS HQ in London, Selby, haggard and pale, with a haunted look in his eyes, reported to Colonel Hacker.

"No," Selby said. "I didn't wait for the results. To be honest, I passed the buck. Told them how to do the job, and ran. If that calls for a court-martial, go ahead."

"Sit down," the colonel said. He opened his desk, and took out a squat, greenish bottle. "Take a slug of this, Lieutenant. You need it—and earned it, according to the French radio."

Selby gulped the bourbon; it was good stuff; the best; a colonel's tipple, in fact.

"Then," he said, a hum in his voice, "Father Placide is …"

"Yes," Hacker said somberly. "He's dead."

"Hurray for me."

"I've no idea how you pulled it off, though. For the record, I ought to know."

"The Threefold Way," Selby said. A large drink on an empty stomach was having its effect.

"Meaning?"

"There was this French kid working on a puzzle, trying to do the impossible—bring gas, water, and electricity from three stations to three houses, without any of the lines crossing. It can't be done—elementary topology. But it gave me the solution.

"There are three ways into every house—gas line, water line, electric line. Civilized houses, anyway," he added.

"We checked out that Father Placide's cell still had a cold-water tap. I got a blueprint of the old plumbing. Easy to tap a water line fifty feet from the building, behind a hedge. We passed word to the other prisoners—if they had water to lay off at a certain time. Got a whole pound of cyanide from a photographer—they use it, you know.

"Injected the stuff into a water pipe before Father Placide had his next meal. No wine, so he was bound to drink a little water with the stale bread—all they gave him. But I didn't wait to find out. So he did it—the poor old man!"

"He did it," Hacker said quietly. "If it helps any," he added, "so did a major of the Gestapo and several guards before they caught on."

Selby poured himself another drink, raised the glass, and looking at the colonel said owlishly, "It's still a damned dirty war—sir!"

"That it is!" said Hacker, reaching for the bottle.

Stalemate

There's an old gag about a gun. Every cartoonist in the country has used it at least once; and it still pops up on TV each time somebody hunts Bugs Bunny or clobbers Quick Draw McGraw.

Well, to me it isn't so funny any more. In fact, I stopped getting humor out of guns at Anzio. When you've seen what a heavy slug can do to the human body, the laughing is over.

And yet, the real irony of the thing is that a situation can be funny and grim at the same time, especially if a guy's lightheaded and thinks his number is up anyway, so what the hell?

That's the way it was in 1945, when we were battling our way into Germany. The Third Reich meant to make a fight of it before yielding any sacred soil of the Fatherland. All of it was rough going, but there was one town—it might have been Aachen—where some real hard-core Nazis held out. My platoon was pinned down tight by fire from a farmhouse. From somewhere inside, above the lower floor, a sharpshooter was keeping our heads in the dirt. He was good, all right; if you raised one ear an inch above dead space, it was nicked by a bullet.

There was no way to flank the place—too much fire power ahead of us left and right. We howled for help to the artillery; they had some one-o-fives behind us in the woods. But you know how it was. Before they had time for a piddling mission like that, the Nazis and us could all die of old age together. There should have been a mortar team available, but an eighty-eight had landed smack in the middle of them the day before, and no replacement had arrived.

So we sweated it out, digging deeper between shots, and trying to get a line on the sniper. It was frustrating as hell, and finally, Sergeant Polanski, in command of my bunch, got fed up and said to me, "Come on, Gordie. I'm gonna get that cute bird the hard way."

Now this Polanski came from Warsaw, and after 1939, no Pole had any love for the Germans. In fact, Polanski was a fanatic, and I didn't hanker to go on the prowl with him into enemy territory. To the rest of us, killing Germans was dirty, unpleasant work which we couldn't squirm out of. But Poley enjoyed it. I didn't blame him for feeling that way, but I wished he'd go it alone.

But you don't argue with rank in the Army, and especially with a hard-nose like Poley. And it helped a little to know that he'd lead the way himself. None of that "you take the point, Private Gordon" stuff.

Well, our guys poured it into that farmhouse with the M-ones and the lone BAR. The Nazi had to keep his head down, and so Poley and I made it to the place without bleeding to death. I covered the rear, while Polanski edged around to the front.

The German had started firing again from upstairs, so Poley sneaked in below, while I did the same from the back door.

But the Nazi must have had ears like a lynx, and heard something. Before we could go up after him, he was coming down to hunt us. Which was fine—in fact, perfect. A lot safer for us to wait, instead of walking down his throat.

I don't know what the German had in mind to behave that way. On the surface, it seemed like a dammed silly stunt for a combat veteran who could shoot so well. He should have mouse-holed instead, or even climbed down the back of the house. Best of all, flipped a grenade down the stairs, if he had one. But anyhow, the minute he saw those polished boots on the stairs, Poley lined up his carbine ready to blast. And the sergeant wasn't about to miss at that range, either.

The German would have been dead in another second, but before Poley could fire, the roof fell in on us. It could have been an eight-eight, or our own one-o-fives suddenly getting into the act at the

158

wrong time, as usual; but something full of TNT crashed into the farm and spoiled everything. I thought sure I was dead. The noise, the tremendous shock, the unbearable flash of light—there's nothing like a shell burst in the parlor to teach a guy he's not here forever.

I don't know how long I was out, but when I came to, my mind was pretty foggy for a while. Then the picture gradually came into focus, and it was weird enough, God knows. I was up to my neck in stones and rubble. Both my legs felt as if they were broken, and should have, because I found out later they were. A few feet from me, Polanski was also pinned down, flat on his belly. There were enough cement blocks and hunks of plaster on his back to flatten an elephant. But he was alive, and trying to squirm free, although without much success, or any hope of it. His left arm was broken—I could tell by the angle—but the right one looked okay.

At first, I didn't even remember about the German we were after, but then a lot of things came back in one rush, because there was this Nazi, a big fellow in an SS uniform, making the third guy in our triangle of lame ducks. He had a huge beam across his left arm just above the elbow. The rest of him was kaput under a heap of junk. I could just see his chin resting on top of the wormy beam, and his cold blue eyes. And that's about all.

Neither man was making a sound, but they were looking at each other. Polanski had brown eyes, and usually they were sort of warm, at least, if you were a friend of his, and hadn't been goofing off. But now they were like some kind of polished stone. The SS had killed Poley's folks, and I guess he hated them more than anything else on God's earth. As for the German, he was a trained hater to begin with.

"You all right, Gordie?" Polanski said.

"I think my legs are broken. I can't move," I told him.

"Neither can I," he grunted, still watching the German. "Luckily, the kraut's in the same boat."

The Nazi glared at both of us, and extended the fingers of his left hand in a clawlike gesture. He couldn't move them very far forward because of that beam crushing his arm above the elbow, but it wouldn't take very much for what he had in mind, and suddenly I had goose pimples. Because there, on the littered floor, all white with plaster, and right between the two men, was Poley's forty-five, which must have fallen out of his holster.

The German had noticed it first, and was trying to reach it. Even though most of him was immobilized, if he could manage to get his left hand on the gun, there was nothing we could do to stop him from shooting us at his leisure. He might need a sighting shot or two, not being able to raise the forty-five to his head, but the range was short— just a few feet. A guy with any sense, knowing the whole American Army was outside of town, would have made a deal and surrendered. But this was a fanatic; an old-line Nazi. If he could shoot us, he sure as hell would, and take his chances with the next patrol. Not many of our guys would kill a man pinned down the way he was, but I'll give him credit for not caring too much either way, if he could just finish off Poley and me.

There wasn't a thing I could do, being far out of reach of the gun; but the sergeant was sure trying. He wriggled and tugged until he actually got his right hand near the automatic. For a minute, I thought he'd even grab it first; but then the Nazi, with a groan, made a mighty stretch that must have nearly dislocated his elbow. I saw one finger brush the butt, coaxing the gun back a fraction of an inch. Polanski was swearing, and it must have been in Polish, all clicks and gutturals. He lunged and snatched out, but it was too late. The German had the forty-five safe in his hand.

It was still awkward for him. In order to get a bead on either of us, he'd have to extend the free part of his arm all the way forward, with the heavy gun tilted at an extreme angle. I figured that even a good shot might miss his first two or three tries from such a position. Even so, that was small comfort; the final result was certain.

Then another idea came. Suppose there was no shell in the chamber? You can't fire an automatic without pulling back the slide, and nobody on earth could do that with one hand. But if there was a slug in the chamber to start, then all the German would have to do was to release the safety catch with his thumb. After the first shot, the others would be chambered by recoil.

I don't know if the Nazi was aware of all this; maybe they didn't teach the GI Colt to SS men, but it didn't matter much. He'd squeeze the trigger, in any case. The gun either would fire, or not. If it worked once, there'd be no hope after that. But if I had my doubts about the readiness of the gun, Polanski didn't. He knew there was a shell in the chamber all ready to go, and that our only chance was to keep it inside. Cursing and moaning with pain, he forced his tortured body out of the rubble a few inches more, just as the German wobbled the gun muzzle roughly into line with the sergeant's head.

And that's why, because of the crazy thing that happened next, whenever I see that silly gag on a TV cartoon, I'm right back in 1945, seeing that big Nazi getting a bead on Poley's head, and remembering how the sergeant made a last desperate lunge and rammed his little finger into the muzzle of the gun.

Believe it or not, I laughed. Lying there with both legs broken, and expecting to be shot up piecemeal, I bellowed with laughter. It was shock and lightheadedness, of course, and I couldn't help it. The whole thing seemed so fantastically silly and nightmarish. Just what good did Poley think he could accomplish by a fool stunt like that?

Then as the Nazi goggled—there's no other word—at him, Polanski gritted in his amateurish German: "*Nicht ein—zwei, schwine—zwei, zwei!*"

Even I could understand that. He was telling the SS man, "If one of us goes, we both go."

And by God, he was right. Poley knew his guns. If you obstruct the barrel in any way, even dip it a quarter of an inch into water, or jam a little snow in the front, the gun will blow up. The gas is in such a hurry to get out that, before it can clear the muzzle, the pressure builds up enough to shatter the whole barrel.

The German was in a bind; he must have understood guns, too. If he pulled the forty-five back out of Poley's reach, it couldn't be aimed, because of the way his elbow was pinned down. And when he pushed it forward long enough to get a bead, there was the sergeant's little finger with its tip in the muzzle.

And the Nazi couldn't even get his head behind the beam and take a chance on getting off with just a mangled hand. Not with his chin rammed tight against the wood and several hundred pounds of assorted rubbish on his back. The way the gun was now, if it exploded, most of his head might go with it.

So it was a Mexican standoff; and when one of our patrols came in an hour later, the two men were still glaring their hatred at one another.

I'll never forget the look on Corporal Slater's face when he saw Poley lying there with his finger in the muzzle of that forty-five.

Yes, it's one of the oldest gags in the business, and I still laugh at it. But I also remember the craziest exhibition of guts and brains—and hate—I've ever seen, when a desperate guy used a silly joke to bluff a killer right out of the game.

The Only Survivor

The only survivor of the infamous Strelsau Massacre, who never before gave a clear, convincing explanation of his miraculous preservation on a battlefield strewn with more than three thousand casualties, died yesterday at the age of eighty-nine, a full general and Hero of the Republic.

This is what he told the priest who gave him the Last Rites:

I'm sure you know, Father—who better than you, so long an apostle of peace and goodwill among all men?—how deep ethnic and religious hatreds run here, and have done so for many bloody centuries.

There I was, after that disastrous battle, bungled by our leaders, several times decorated for valor, a newly-made captain, youngest in the corps, lying on the ground, helpless, with a shell-fragment in my thigh, completely unable to move rapidly, if at all.

Next to me, without so much as a bruise, was Plavinicic, the butt of his company. He was a very bad soldier, I have to tell you; timid, even cowardly, wearing a slovenly uniform without any grace or panache, with a dirty rifle he could never aim right, even if he had the guts to fire it at anybody, which I doubt. He objected to killing, in fact.

But we were trapped together, certainly doomed, with the sea at our backs and the merciless irregulars moving in from the other three sides to exterminate us. No quarter was ever given in these terrible battles; all the survivors, wounded or not, were dispatched, usually with a bullet in the head.

Now this Plavinicic, as I've said, was a nothing, a weedy youth, a third-rate actor by profession, who fancied himself an artist, heir to Olivier, no less; what a fool!

He was totally useless in a fight, had no discipline or loyalty to our country, nor did he even hate our age-old foes. Yes, despite all that, so desperate were we for infantrymen that we conscripted the boy, no matter how he protested, whined, and even sobbed.

But worthless as he was, Plavinicic had hit upon an amazingly cunning stratagem, prompted by a part in some silly play, ironically titled, "The Captain's Trick." It involved the use of a cleverly made patch, made of some flesh-colored plastic with a most realistic looking bloody bullet-hole in the center. In the play, the captain had fitted it to his forehead to feign death and so win the sympathy from a chit of a girl he coveted. A libel on the military!

Anyhow, after being conscripted, Plavinicic stole the prop and took it with him to the army, having some vague idea of using it in his first combat to play dead and escape the killing-ground. Most ingenious, I have to admit, however defeatist and cowardly.

So there we were, hopelessly trapped, with the enemy troops quartering the area, pistols in hand, to give us all the *coup de grâce*. I had to watch, enviously, I concede, as Plavinicic, with his invariable little smirk, attached the patch to his forehead and assumed a convincing sprawl, obviously a dead soldier. And I, with my damned injured thigh, a real fighter with a fine future, much to offer the Fatherland, and very likely a general's stars before the age of fifty.

And now the part so hard to tell—but I must tell it if I'm to hope for absolution—isn't that so, Father? But I remind you, too, that he was never a comrade, a fellow-in-arms, but a cowardly conscript, and not even of our faith, but practically a heretic who often scoffed at things sacred. He was skinny and weak; my hands and arms were very strong, muscular, not as you see them now, so wasted after many years.

Yes, God forgive me, I strangled him and took the patch. I had to kill him, you must understand; craven that he was, Plavinicic would have betrayed me to the first enemy soldier who came by to finish us off. He was not the kind to die alone even if I'd not taken his patch. He cared nothing about my value to the army and his homeland.

At dusk I crept slowly, painfully away and made it to our own lines. I die a general, a hero, but I have not had an easy moment these sixty-odd years.

Now, Father, I beg you, give me absolution …

The Most Dangerous
Animal in the World

When I was a young boy—it was a very long time ago, and much has become blurry in my memory, but not important events—a man in my little town of Pacific Grove, California, claimed to have a live specimen of the most dangerous animal in the world. This was a most remarkable assertion, obviously, and one that the adults, though a very Bohemian bunch in those days, didn't take seriously. As poets and artists themselves, they were given to tall tales.

We kids weren't so skeptical, mainly because the man lived near the 17 Mile Village in a big, ramshackle house that was crammed with the most exciting things we'd ever seen or heard of. There were dozens of mounted heads: lions, tigers, bears, Cape buffalo, rhinos, and others I don't remember. And what weapons! He had rifles (such as the Tower musket he loved) that dated back to long-forgotten colonial wars, grenades, mortars, sabers too heavy for most of us to swing, glittering dress swords, knives, daggers, the odd, crooked blades of Gurkha warriors, and some weapons probably never used in battle but superbly engraved and inlaid, often in gold. But the old man—his name was Arthur Johnson—had a few favorites of his own, like the huge, double-barreled English elephant gun (which fired a

.600 caliber solid slug) and his cherished buffalo killer of the West, a massive Sharps.

He had accumulated all these things over a long, nomadic life of travel, exploration, hunting, and mercenary activities for a variety of governments, most headed, he assured us, by scoundrels. We were particularly fascinated by a Masai spear (stained with what Johnson said was lion's blood), which he hung on the wall with a giant shield of tough, thick bull's hide. It was, he explained, the only protection a young would-be warrior was allowed when he went out to prove himself by killing one of the great cats single-handed. Awed as we were then, I now know we didn't really appreciate the courage that must've taken. Watching today's marvelous wildlife programs on TV, many people are seeing for the first time what only a few travelers saw in my day: the unbelievable power, speed, and agility of a male lion, with those great masses of shoulder muscle pumping as he runs down a wildebeest, zebra, or even a highly dangerous buffalo. The shield he showed us had obviously been scarred by terrible claws.

Johnson had lost his wife, Caroline, decades earlier to some mysterious tropical disease—or so we inferred, since he never discussed her. He had no children and was probably a bit lonely. He seemed to enjoy our youthful boisterousness.

We usually visited him on Saturday nights so we could stay fairly late, entranced by his dramatically told stories. It was only after many sessions with us that he remarked, almost casually one evening, that up in the attic he had a live specimen of the most dangerous animal in the world. How or where he'd obtained it, he wouldn't say, but he hinted that such possession was illegal and that our silence on the matter would be appreciated. We figured that meant to keep this information from the authorities, not our parents. We couldn't imagine how such a creature—naturally we thought of the great predators—could really be confined in anybody's attic. Our folks, reasonably enough, scoffed at the idea. But they knew Johnson to be a remarkable man, one who could back up his most outrageous tales with unimpeachable documents—letters, awards, newspaper accounts, and even some official histories.

Of course, the questions flew. Was it a tiger? A lion? A polar bear? Though we were certain they couldn't dwell so silently in a small room overhead, we still had to ask. The list of obvious suspects was soon exhausted, but some more sophisticated queries came from Maxie Landau, our resident nerd, although that word was unknown then. In fact, it's a bit unfair, since even though he was a whiz at math and science, he also had an unerring eye, whether with darts, a BB gun, a slingshot, or the .22 pistol his father allowed him to shoot under supervision. He had what I now realize was a skeptical, ironic intellect none of us then appreciated. Now he's famous for solving the thorny mathematical conjecture of Goldbach (which states that every even number is the sum of two primes, a very knotty problem that baffled the best researchers for over two centuries), and those of his pals who, like me, still survive can smugly say we expected it!

It was he who first suggested, after we'd run out of possibilities from among the lower animals, that since man himself is demonstrably the most dangerous critter cavorting about this earth, Mr. Johnson had a slave chained up there in the attic, probably a mass murderer he'd secretly captured during one of his adventures and brought back in triumph, not to be turned over to the law but as a kind of testament and trophy. Half-amused and half-indignant, the old man vehemently denied this charge.

Maxie then shifted to the matter of just how to define the word *animal*, a point none of us had considered. That was easy, Johnson told him: anything alive that isn't a plant. So the young skeptic asked his next question: Is a person merely a super-animal or something qualitatively different, an exalted being with a unique soul that no other organism has? In a small town in those days, Darwin was pretty much beyond the pale, and it took a bold spirit indeed to agree with him that people had actually developed over millions of years from worms, lizards, and—horrors!—apelike beasts.

However, the old man didn't flinch but sturdily assured us that humans were only a kind of animal, though not the top killer in the attic.

That led to many other related queries, often repeated in exasperation but with no satisfactory replies from the infuriating eccentric. For example, what about noise, none of which ever emanated from upstairs while we were in the house. Did the beast roar, snarl, growl, grunt, or hiss?

"Of course," Johnson assured us. "Most living things do. This creature isn't very loud, but it can terrify in the right circumstances, and the sound can jerk the bravest man or woman from a sound sleep."

When Maxie had grown tired of this fruitless ritual, he noted the growing number of car-crash casualties and asked if the Model T auto might be some kind of animal. It was getting ever more dangerous, he added, smirking.

We constantly pestered the old man for a glimpse of the deadly beast but to no avail. He'd just smile enigmatically and refuse, giving no reason, which naturally made us suspect that the creature was so aggressive and powerful that if upset by a bunch of excited kids, it might escape, slaughter the lot of us, and then rage through the town, killing everybody in sight before taking to the hills.

We drove poor Mrs. Herrick, our local librarian, nearly crazy with questions about whatever rare beasts might infest distant countries. We asked about snakes in Thailand, giant bats in South America, and even those huge, lumbering, nasty Komodo dragons of the Spice Islands. She was able to turn up nothing that satisfied Johnson, and the riddle remained unsolved. Whatever answers we did get from the old man were maddeningly ambiguous or vague. When we asked how many people were actually killed yearly by the nameless beast, he merely smiled and said, "Lots."

Susie Wright was annoyed by this and challenged him for the first time. "How many is 'lots'?" she demanded. "A hundred? A thousand?"

He stared at her, maliciously amused. "How about a million, Susie?" he deadpanned.

I broke in. "You're kidding. You gotta be."

"Not so fast," Maxie said. "We forgot the cobras in India. They kill an awful lot, I've read."

Johnson frowned. "Nowhere near that many," he snapped.

We probably should have given up and simply ignored him until he got sick of our neglect and told us. But we kept coming back for more pointless, frustrating sessions until, finally, full of a desperation born partly of small-town boredom, we violated the trust between Johnson and us.

On a day when we knew he'd be off to the county seat on some matter involving his property, a small group of us—the most daring and angry—slipped into his house via a basement window and surged up to the attic, resolved to get the answer no matter what.

We found the door closed and padlocked, but we'd come well prepared to break and enter. Yet standing there, we couldn't help feeling apprehensive. We listened for any telltale sounds—growls, snarls, whatever; surely the thing wasn't mute. And we hoped it was restrained by heavy chains or thick steel bars.

Finally Elmer Grain, the biggest and strongest of our bunch, one who never said much but was given to action quite readily, slipped a crowbar into the padlock's hoop and, with one powerful wrench, broke it free.

We were now able to go in, but we waited, each wanting someone else to be first. But nobody wanted to back out, either, so somebody, I forget who, pushed the door open, and we all charged in, feeling safety in numbers perhaps.

The small, gloomy room was cluttered with all sorts of stuff Johnson hadn't bothered to display, but there was a relatively clear space in the center where a little table stood. On it was a big glass jar. Puzzled but still a bit scared, we moved closer and peered inside. We saw a dry twig on the bottom, and that seemed to be all.

"Hey," Maxie blurted, "there's nothing here. What is this? Is Mr. Johnson crazy or just fooling us?"

But he was wrong; the container wasn't empty after all. Perched almost invisible on the twig was a tiny insect with dainty, spotted wings. It was poised at an angle from the horizontal, like a miniature plane ready to take off. And it was definitely alive, shifting its position slightly at our noisy intrusion.

It was only then that we noticed the neatly printed card attached to the glass. It read, "ANOPHELES, THE MALARIA MOSQUITO. THE MOST DANGEROUS ANIMAL IN THE WORLD!"

You know the funny part? It was true then, over seventy years ago, and it's still true today. As they say, you can look it up.

The Miracle of the Bread

This is the true story about how I deliberately, rashly, violated a taboo, and saved my mother's life. The taboo was never spelled out, or taken from the Bible, and had no force of law behind it, but was nevertheless very strong, as small-town traditions tend to be. This one was rarely broken, and never before by a kid.

It happened a very long time ago, Christmas Eve in 1925, to be specific, a tragic time for my small family. My mother, struggling mightily against high odds to raise me, then ten years old, and my younger sister, seven, Cele. My father, who had worked all his life in a steel-mill at a difficult, highly dangerous job, had died in an accident involving a terrible spill of molten metal, leaving the three of us utterly lost, bewildered, sad, and lacking money even for the basics of life.

My mother, Susan, while filling a big copper basin with boiling water, preparatory to doing our laundry, splashed some of the fluid on her right arm, badly scalding it. That was the way clothes were cleaned then—boiling water and bars of yellow soap called Fels Naptha, I think. Although small and rather frail, she had always managed to handle the tedious, laborious chore as most women did in a world without washing machines. But worn out and depressed over her recent loss and the awful responsibilities it brought, she failed to concentrate on what she was doing and sustained a third-degree burn.

It didn't seem too bad at first, and our doctor, gruff, but actually very kind, said it would probably heal if cold compresses were continuously applied. But, alas, not so. Whether her resistance was low after all she'd just been through, or it was a bit of bad luck, the wound soon became a really nasty ulcer that wouldn't heal and might end in gangrene. Dr. Grant brought in, even though he himself was unlikely to get paid except by our fervent gratitude, a specialist from Chicago. But he had nothing to offer but a dubious treatment tried in World War I, Carrel-Dakin Solution, which was basically a chlorine bleach mix supposed to sterilize and heal such injuries. On a scald it was completely useless, even harmful. Death and disease from infections were common then; there were no antibiotics whatever. Either the patient's own body fought off the disease, or it was the end. My mother, I knew with dreadful certainty, was doomed.

Full of despair, I roamed the snowy streets wondering what miracle I could invoke to save her, but what could I, a boy of ten, knowing nothing about medicine, do? It was then that I ran into an acquaintance of mine, a red-haired kid about my own age, a sort of Huckleberry Finn, who lived on his own like a stray dog, distrustful of all adults, and with every bad habit available to children in those more innocent days. He said little, and, it was thought, bathed less. Nobody had ever been able to keep him in school, even in 1925 when adults made and enforced, they liked to think, the rules. He had, in a way, a kind of invisibility; one minute he was there in plain sight, the next, and he was gone, nobody could say where. Of course, we were repeatedly warned to steer clear of him, but he fascinated us, and so we always managed to meet him "accidentally." Although rarely seen in public, as noted, he seemed to know everything that went on in town.

And for sure, all knew he was a good-hearted kid, and being almost an orphan himself, having fled from an abusive, alcoholic father and weak, silly mother, I thought he could fully understand my grief.

When I poured out all my despair and hopelessness, he reflected briefly, then said, "Why not try the old witch?" He was referring to a Miz Buffington, a quirky recluse who had moved here from England years ago. She lived in a big, ramshackle house near the woods at the edge of town, and was often called upon by folks who distrusted or couldn't afford doctors. She was said to be very ugly—in fact, one quip about her was that she had fallen from the Ugly Tree and hit every branch on the way down. But oddly, she had a voice like honey dripping from a comb, although it spoke, very ungrammatically in some kind of British dialect. But she knew every medicinal plant—there were many—in the woods, and sold them for pennies along with sound advice on their proper use.

"What can she do?" I asked bleakly. "She's just a crazy old woman. That's what they say, and I'm not supposed to ever go near her; nobody is."

"You just bet she ain't. She knows lots of stuff doctors don't. Herbs,"—he pronounced the "h"—"roots, leaves, mushrooms, bark; hey, she cured me of some really big warts on my hand."

I was not a rebel, unlike my advisor, but with my mother's life in the balance, I'd consult anybody, taboo or not. It wasn't easy, since I'd been taught to do as told by adults who always knew best. In fact, I took the long route to Miz Buffington's place, prolonging the confrontation I feared. What if she too could do nothing?

When I did get to her house, almost invisible among the trees, the front door was wide open, and I saw a huge, shadowy room, a place full of gloom, not a light on, and cluttered with many boxes, bales, barrels, and loaded tables. There were puzzling things hanging from the ceiling which I couldn't see clearly. I knocked timidly on the jamb, and getting no response, again, more loudly.

Then a silvery, sweet, melodic little voice sang, "Hut, boy, who be ye and what wantin' o' me?" and a shriveled, tiny old woman appeared. She was indeed very ugly, with a face, I thought, like a moldy walnut, all cracks, furrows, and wrinkles. But suddenly I lost all fear of her, and, in truth, felt a rush of hope. Apparently she had what we call today "presence," a strong, almost overwhelming individuality. When she noted somehow that I had tapped with an inquiring finger a grotesque little figure hanging by the door—it combined a large fishtail with the upper half of a mummified child, I thought—she chuckled and said, "They call that there a Jenny Haniver. They made 'em hundreds o' years ago. Sewed a fishtail to half a monkey. Clever job o' stitchin'. Ye can't find the seam. Fooled even some o' them high-an'-mighty perfessers thinkin' they was true mermaids!"

She motioned me in then with a quick, peremptory wave of one hand, and I expected some lights to be turned on, but not so. The bright winter sky, however, lit up her face, and I saw a pair of amazing eyes, huge and soft and brown and warm as melted caramel. I realized, looking at them, that she was blind. Just how she knew I was a boy and had tapped the fake mermaid, I can't be sure. My light step, perhaps, or my uncertain young voice. I was pretty clean for a kid back then with no showers, but maybe had a faint woodsy smell in my clothes; a boy smell. Probably, as with most blind people, her other senses had become much stronger. But it doesn't matter; she knew.

"Hut, boy—yer name."

"I'm Alan Wright."

"Son o' Susan, hey? The small, quick, pretty one. Minds me, that one, o' a hummin'bird. A real nice lady, not like some hereabouts."

"Yes," I said glumly, thinking of her lying there in bed so pale and still, hoping for a miracle, more for Cele and me than herself as Death flew low over her wasted little body. Luckily, one of several kind neighbors, Caroline Johnson, was looking after her, giving up her own Christmas Eve. She was a former Southern Belle, still charming after sixty years in the North. She and the others often brought us food and similar necessities we were so short of.

"What d'ye want, boy? Better, what d'ye need; there's a big difference. I don't deal much in selfish wants. They're usually not worth havin'."

Quickly, my words tumbling over each other, I blurted out the whole dismal story. She listened silently, her face a mask. Then, still without a word, she went to the back of the room where I could barely make out her small body, and picked up a basket full of vague, irregular shapes I couldn't identify. She put some of them in a big bowl, added what I guessed was water, and vigorously mashed them into a paste. When she brought the stuff to me, I saw it was greenish and smelled moldy, a bit like wet seaweed.

175

"Put several tablespoons o' this here into the ulcer three times a day," she ordered me. "Might help, I shouldn't wonder." She paused, then added cryptically, "'ut's Healin' Bread."

That didn't sound like a strong endorsement of the medication, but nevertheless, I don't know why, I felt a great burden had been lifted from my heart.

I thanked her fervently, but she just nodded her head, saying in the bell-like voice, "Yer a good boy, an' all will be merry yet—Merry Christmas, boy."

The rest of the story can be quite short. Ignoring Cele's bratty young remarks, I spread the green mush into the huge ulcer as directed, and within twenty-four hours there was an unbelievable change for the better. The oozing stopped; the redness began to fade, replaced by the healthy pink called granulation; and the deadly bacteria, almost certainly staphlococcus, were literally massacred by a new, indomitable foe never before used on them. They had no defense against it.

Looking back now from the 21st Century—which I never expected to see!—I think I know what happened. Those chunks were just moldy bread, but what a mold! It must have been Penicillium, the miraculous stuff noted first by Tyndall, the great 19th century physicist, and much later isolated and concentrated by the British bacteriologist, Fleming.

To those 1925 germs it was totally deadly, and it wiped them out in all their teeming millions. Mother had a long, happy life, and we never forgot what Miz Buffington had done for us. While the "old witch" lived, there was nothing we wouldn't do for her. Now, in 2004, I still marvel at the lovely spirit in that small, valiant body.

Checklist of Sources

The checklist below gives the original publication source for each of the stories included in this collection:

"Treed by Terror," previously unpublished.
"Weeping Willie," previously unpublished.
"An Unlicensed Surgeon," previously unpublished.
"Reconstruction," first published in *Escapade*, January 1956.
"Masterpiece," first published in *Escapade*, September 1956.
"Morning After," previously unpublished.
"Night of the Puppet," previously unpublished.
"Man's Best Friend," previously unpublished.
"Secret Vice," first published in *The Evening News and Star*, September 19, 1962.
"The Drum Major," first published in *Alfred Hitchcock's Mystery Magazine*, February 1962.
"The Crime," first published in *Romper*, Vol. 1, No. 2, 1965.
"A Letter from Réjane," previously unpublished.
"Birthday in a Garden," previously unpublished.
"The Odyssey of Epeira," first published (as "Eight Legged Monster") in *Boys' Life*, August 1952.
"The Black Tyrant," first published in *Boys' Life*, September 1955.
"The Fiery Patriot," first published in *Argosy*, April 1965.
"The Room," first published in *Argosy*, September 1965.
"Dressed to Kill," first published in *Argosy*, November 1965.
"Last Gasp," first published in *Argosy*, February 1966.
"Murder of a Priest," first published in *Ellery Queen's Mystery Magazine*, September 1967.
"Stalemate," first published in *Argosy*, October 1961.
"The Only Survivor," first published in *Ellery Queen's Mystery Magazine*, May 1994.
"The Most Dangerous Animal in the World," first published in *Cricket*, August 1999.
"The Miracle of the Bread," previously unpublished.

About the Author

Arthur Porges was born in Chicago, Illinois on August 20, 1915. One of four brothers, he was educated at Roosevelt High School and Senn High School before enrolling at The Lewis Institute where he achieved a Bachelor of Science Degree in Mathematics. After the successful completion of his postgraduate studies, through which he attained Masters Degrees in Mathematics and Engineering from the Illinois Institute of Technology, Porges enlisted in the U.S. Army in 1942. During the Second World War he served as an artillery instructor, teaching algebra and trigonometry to field personnel. He was stationed at various military installations including Camp White in Oregon, Fort Sill, Oklahoma, Camp Roberts, California and at Barnes Hospital in Vancouver, Washington. After the war Porges returned to Illinois and taught mathematics at the Western Military Academy, going on to serve as an assistant professor at De Paul University. Having taught at Occidental College in Los Angeles for a brief stint in the late forties, Porges made a permanent move to California in 1951 and spent several years as a mathematics teacher at Los Angeles City College. During this period he wrote and sold short stories as a sideline. In 1957, Porges retired from teaching to write full-time. He went on to publish hundreds of short stories in numerous magazines and newspapers. Many of his stories appeared in *Alfred Hitchcock's Mystery Magazine*, *Ellery Queen's Mystery Magazine*, *Amazing Stories* and *The Magazine of Fantasy and Science Fiction*. His fiction spanned several genres, with tales ranging from science fiction and fantasy to horror, mysteries, and so on. At his most prolific his work was appearing in three or four periodicals in one month alone. Among his best known stories are "The Ruum," "The Rats," "No Killer Has Wings," "The Mirror" and "The Rescuer." Five previous book collections of his short stories have been published: *Three Porges Parodies and a Pastiche* (1988), *The Mirror and Other Strange Reflections* (2002), *Eight Problems in Space: The Ensign De Ruyter Stories* (2008), *The Adventures of Stately Homes and Sherman Horn* (2008) and *The Calabash of Coral Island and Other Early Stories* (2008). A keen birdwatcher and an avid reader, Porges also wrote many articles, essays and poems, most of which were published in the *Monterey Herald*. After spells in Laguna Beach and San Clemente, Porges moved north, eventually settling in Pacific Grove. He passed away, at the age of 90, in May 2006.